Welcome to the November 2008 collection of
Harlequin Presents! What better way to warm up
in the coming winter months than with a hot novel
from your favorite Presents author—and this month
we have plenty in-store to keep you cozy! Don't miss
Ruthlessly Bedded by the Italian Billionaire
by Emma Darcy, in which a case of mistaken identity
leads Jenny Kent to a billionaire's bed. Plus, be sure
to look out for *The Sheikh's Wayward Wife*,
the second installment of Sandra Marton's fantastic
trilogy THE SHEIKH TYCOONS, and Robyn Donald's
final story in her brilliant MEDITERRANEAN PRINCES
duet, *The Mediterranean Prince's Captive Virgin*.

Also this month, read the story of sexy Italian
Joe Mendez and single mom Rachel in *Mendez's
Mistress* by favorite author Anne Mather. And in
Kate Walker's *Bedded by the Greek Billionaire*,
a gorgeous Greek seeks revenge on an English rose—
by making her his mistress! Vincenzo is intent
on claiming his son from estranged wife Emma
in *Sicilian Husband, Unexpected Baby* by
Sharon Kendrick, while Susan Napier brings you
Public Scandal, Private Mistress, in which
unsuspecting Veronica becomes involved with
billionaire Luc. Finally, in Ally Blake's *A Night with the
Society Playboy*, Caleb wants just one more night with
the woman who walked out on him ten years ago....

We'd love to hear what you think about Presents.
E-mail us at Presents@hmb.co.uk or join in the
discussions at www.iheartpresents.com and
www.sensationalromance.blogspot.com, where you'll
also find more information about books and authors!

EXCLUSIVELY HIS

Back in his bed—and he's better than ever!

Whether you shared his bed for one night or five years, certain men are impossible to forget! He might be your ex, but when you're back in his bed, the passion is not just hot, it's scorching!

That's how it is for the couples in this brand-new miniseries from Harlequin Presents. He really is better than ever, at least in the bedroom…. Last time it didn't work out. This time everything is different. But hold on tight—in these stories it's going to be an emotional, passionate, heart-stopping ride!

Look out for more EXCLUSIVELY HIS novels from Harlequin Presents in 2009!

Susan Napier

PUBLIC SCANDAL, PRIVATE MISTRESS

EXCLUSIVELY HIS

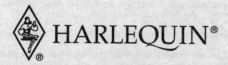
HARLEQUIN®

TORONTO • NEW YORK • LONDON
AMSTERDAM • PARIS • SYDNEY • HAMBURG
STOCKHOLM • ATHENS • TOKYO • MILAN • MADRID
PRAGUE • WARSAW • BUDAPEST • AUCKLAND

ISBN-13: 978-0-373-12777-1
ISBN-10:   0-373-12777-4

PUBLIC SCANDAL, PRIVATE MISTRESS

First North American Publication 2008.

www.eHarlequin.com

Printed in U.S.A.

CHAPTER ONE

SHE could always blame Paris.

Glorious, graceful, flagrant and flamboyant, tantalising, *Paris*...

City of lovers, whose very air was romantic intoxication to breathe—a potent brew that ravished the senses and excited the blood. Just to *be* in Paris was a heady invitation to recklessness.

And Paris on Bastille Day was even more of an enticement to shed the shackles of convention and be bold, free-thinking and daring. Celebrating the spirit of rebellion, the entire city had been in a euphoric mood, the sweltering summer heat-wave adding a sultry edge to the holiday atmosphere, tourists and residents alike thronging the streets and partying far into the steamy night. Behaving with reckless abandon and getting swept away in the passion of the moment had seemed to be an essential part of the whole experience.

Oh, yes, Paris was definitely to blame. After all, what defence did a lone, inexperienced Kiwi traveller have against the sophisticated wiles of the most seductive city in the world?

Veronica Bell slowly eased open the French doors that screened off the bedroom from the rest of the small apartment and tiptoed across the polished oak floorboards, clutching her strappy sandals and gossamer-fine crocheted wrap against her chest. At a shade under six foot, and of queenly proportions, she was acutely aware that she wasn't built for stealth. She could feel her heart skittering nervously beneath the thin silk of her camisole top as she paused to orientate herself and received her second major shock of the morning: her purse was no longer where she had left it.

Or, rather, where she *thought* she had put it down.

Veronica had to admit that her exact recollection of events was somewhat scrambled by the mind-blowing climax to her last night in the French capital. She raked sleep-tangled mahogany locks away from her damp forehead, forcing down a fresh surge of panic at the thought of the outrageous risks she had taken.

Right now she needed to focus on the most urgent problem— which was getting out of here with her dignity intact.

It was barely dawn, faint streaks of pale light only just beginning to creep in around the edges of the heavy, cream-coloured drapes drawn across the row of double-glazed windows facing out over the street. She was starting to think that she might have to risk turning on a light when she suddenly caught a sight of a tell-tale glint in the thick pile of the shaggy floor rug. She crouched and fished out the slender, black-sequinned shoulder bag, which had fallen from the side arm of the low-slung couch and was half hidden behind the chunky square leg.

Her anxious fingertips traced the reassuring shape of her passport and folded money-belt through the pliant exoskeleton of overlapping sequins.

Thank God! She banished the mortifying vision of trying to explain how she had come to lose all her travel documents and money to a cynical *gendarme*, or some smirking official at the New Zealand Embassy.

Rising to her feet, she added the bag to the top of the bundle in her arms and began tiptoeing the last few metres to the apartment door.

A whispery rustle behind her, accompanied by a low, throaty sound, like the warning purr of a dangerous predator, made her freeze to the spot.

She looked back with a thrill of apprehension.

A gap in the curtains had thrown a long, pale yellow finger of light across the floor, pointing to the source of the sound. Through the square glass panes of the French doors she had left slightly ajar, Veronica had a slanting view of the king-sized bed and the big, rangy, suntanned male body sprawled face-up in a tangle of white cotton sheets.

The throaty rumble sounded again and she watched with guilty fascination as lean, muscled limbs thrashed free of the entwining sheets, flashing rippling shoulders, bulging biceps and hard flanks, glistening with perspiration. No wonder he was hot—with no air-conditioning the apartment was stiflingly warm—but temperature wasn't the only reason the word came to mind.

Stripped, he really was incredibly gorgeous, she marvelled with a renewed sense of awe. Even more attractive than he had been in his stylishly scruffy jeans and white designer tee shirt.

It was hard to believe that she had succeeded in snaring such a prime specimen for a starring role in her rosy, romantic fantasy of a love affair in Paris. Only it had been lust rather than love, she reminded herself sternly, which had directed the script. Her frothy romantic comedy had unexpectedly turned into an adrenalin-spiked action-adventure…and the hero had more than lived up to his billing!

His dark head jerked on the pillow, and Veronica's pulse kicked into overdrive. Heat pumped through her veins, her body tightening with defensive tension, her mouth going dry as she tried to think of something to say that was in character with the woman she had pretended to be, something witty and insouciant, and appropriate to the occasion…

But what?

Unfortunately, all her former boldness had deserted her the moment she opened her eyes and reality sank in. She hadn't intended to fall asleep. Her private fantasising had always stopped short of the uncomfortable practicalities of the morning after.

Her brief flare of panic faded as she realised his restless movements were only a prelude to him turning over in a long, shuddering, stretch and roll of the impressive body, which left her staring at his naked back, his sleepy grumble muffled into silence as he laced his arm under the empty pillow beside him—still bearing the blurred imprint of her head—and drew it to his chest, burying his face in its billowing softness. His thick mane of silky-straight jet-black hair fanned out across the top of his hunched shoulders, his powerful musculature rippling under tawny skin as he melted back into stillness like a lazy, well-satiated lion, totally secure in his innate supremacy.

The animal comparison brought a flush of memory to Veronica's cheeks, an invisible souvenir to sigh over when she was old and grey, or even a month hence, when she was back in wintry-wet Auckland, struggling to make a success of her ideas, and in need of proof that she had the courage and audacity to make her dreams come true.

She scurried to the deadlocked door, grimacing at the metallic clunk made by the weighty bolt as she finally wrenched it open.

She couldn't resist a final, fleeting peek over her shoulder, however, and carried off a vivid image of bare, male buttocks erotically framed in a twisted skein of sheet, the superbly toned muscles pulled taut by his drawn-up knees, revealing a sexy hint of dark fluff on the underside of the smoothly sculpted globes where they curved into the tops of his strong, hair-roughened thighs.

Distracted, she let the heavy door go too soon, and it shut with a bang that reverberated up and down the empty stairwell.

The sound was magnified by her twanging nerves into a sonic boom and she plunged down the stairs, her bare feet slapping against the wooden treads. Reaching the second-floor landing, she dug blindly into her bundled-up purse and, miraculously, the small metal key with its numbered tag fell straight into her hand, but her fingers were shaking so much that she had difficulty trying to slot it into the door of her rented apartment. She cursed under her breath, her ears alert for prowling footsteps from above.

She didn't want to risk him finding out where she was staying. He had no idea that the holiday rental she had referred to with deliberate vagueness at the start of the evening as being 'in the Marais' was literally right under his very nose.

She had bubbled with secret amusement when he had swept her back to his lair in the early hours of the morning, but thankfully a tiny, remaining spark of common sense had kept her from blurting out her startled recognition as he had paused to punch in the keycode at the entrance to a graceful old building in the historic rue de Birague.

Still on a champagne-fuelled high, and abuzz with excitement after their thrilling escape from the near-riot a few blocks away in the Place de la Bastille, she had embraced the fantastic coincidence as kismet…a serendipitous sign that they were fated to fulfil a passionate destiny.

Of course, in the sober light of day, the coincidence seemed a great deal less karmic given the fact that they had first encountered each other in the tiny Latin American bar just across the street from the apartments—the kind of place that was more of a hang-out for local residents and workers than a magnet for the passing tourist trade.

Once inside the apartment, her knees turned to water, and she slumped limply back against the door, biting back a giggle of semi-hysterical relief, her hand instinctively going to the small pendant of New Zealand jade, carved in the shape of a stylised Maori fishhook, that she always wore around her neck. To her dismay the reassuring touch of home was no longer there. Her fingers spread over her bare breastbone as she realised with a sharp pang that it must still be somewhere in Luc's apartment, lost to her for ever, for there was no way she was going back for it.

She was certainly racking up a lot of memorable firsts in the first week of her trip: first time on a plane, first visit to London, first experience of being sick and alone in a country where she didn't speak the language...

First time she had woken up with a sexy stranger.

She quickly pushed the alarming notion aside. 'No regrets' was what she had decided in the heat of passion, and she intended to stick to her bargain.

Besides, he wasn't a *complete* stranger, she corrected herself, instantly breaching her self-imposed ban. In spite of the language barrier they had worked out a way to communicate.

Lucien.

Luc.

The intimate shortening of his name made her shiver. She remembered laughing it when he had first kissed her in the jam-packed Champs-de-Mars from where they had watched the elaborate fireworks display at the Trocadéro, and sighing it during their scorching embrace behind a pillar in the Place des Vosges.

Her dreaming dove-grey eyes suddenly caught sight of the digital glow of the clock on the microwave in the kitchen alcove and she gave a squawk as she confirmed the time with a horrified glance at the watch on her winter-pale wrist.

She scrambled around the one-bedroomed apartment, flinging her scattered possessions into the open suitcase on the floor. She wasn't even going to have time for a lightning shower, she realised, swapping her skirt and top for khaki cargo shorts and a yellow ribbed singlet and scooping up her toiletries from the bathroom. She ducked to look in the rectangular mirror, positioned annoyingly low on the wall, and gasped at the sight of her haystack hair, the powdery black smudges of mascara under her eyes and sprinkle of freckles shining through the patchy foundation on her forehead and shiny nose.

Another reason to be thankful that Lucien was a heavy sleeper! she thought, using a tissue to scrape off a hasty application of cleanser and following it up with a quick swipe of SPF moisturiser and lipstick.

She brushed her hair with a ruthless speed that brought tears to her eyes, gathering the subtly layered strands into a simple pony-tail high on the back of her head, the ends skimming the bare skin at the top of her spine.

Just over an hour later she was pelting down one of the long, outside platforms at the Gare de Lyon to join the rapidly vanishing queue for the first high-speed train of the day to Avignon with only a few minutes to spare, her wheeled suitcase jouncing along behind her, the strap from her heavy cabin bag biting into her shoulder as she held out her ticket to be checked.

Predictably for the way her morning was going, her carriage turned out to be almost at the front of the extra-long train, and her leg muscles began to pull as she increased the pace of her fast trot.

The train was already packed, the annual summer exodus of Parisians out of the city having obviously begun, and Veronica had trouble finding a space in the baggage racks when she hauled her suitcase up the narrow stairs to the upper compartment and finally sank gratefully into her seat. Travelling alone could be extremely stressful, she was discovering, even when you were fiercely determined to enjoy every moment of it. Unfortunately she had no one with whom to share the highs and lows of travel, the awe and excitement of being out in the big, wide world after years of merely dreaming about it.

She looked at the unoccupied window-seat beside her, and shifted into it. If Karen had been with her, as planned, they would have been laughing about being late for the train, instead of worrying about it.

Part of her was still furious with her younger sister for wrecking their holiday plans.

When she had flown into Heathrow a week ago from Auckland, Veronica had been confidently expecting twenty-year-old Karen to be at the airport to greet her with a hug, full of plans for a fun weekend in London before they boarded the Eurostar to Paris for the start of their French holiday together.

Instead, she had hung around for forty minutes in the arrivals hall before getting anxious. Used to Karen's chronic lateness, she had suddenly remembered to switch on her cell phone, but when the prepaid global roaming had finally chosen to glom onto a compatible network, there were no messages showing, so she had texted off a hopeful 'where r u?' in case they were simply missing each other in the ebb and flow of the airport.

The reply, when it came, had turned her eager anticipation to weary disappointment.

'Sorry. Can u get taxi? Wil explain when u get here.'

It had better be a good explanation, Veronica had brooded. After twenty-six hours of so-called 'direct' economy-class flight, which included two drawn-out stopovers in featureless transit lounges, and a few more free glasses of wine on the plane than she ought, she had been feeling extremely washed out. However, she had boosted her flagging energies with the cheering knowledge of good times ahead, and had geared herself up to make her own way to the serviced flat in Kensington where Karen's employer, who had departed on holiday the previous day, had left her assistant to enjoy the last weekend of the expiring lease.

Typically for Karen—who consistently spent more than she earned—she hadn't factored cost into her blithe suggestion of a taxi. It probably hadn't even occurred to her that her sister might be on a strict budget, Veronica had thought, her accountant's soul cringing as she mentally translated the quoted fare into New Zealand dollars. In spite of her creeping jet lag, she had decided to take the cheaper option of the underground, emerging battered but triumphant from the thick of the morning rush hour, within walking distance of the address marked on her pocket map.

When her sister had thrown open the door of the flat and welcomed her with the much-delayed hug, all petty annoyances had fled…for a while.

'At last!' Karen declared, her green eyes bright with suppressed excitement as she helped carry in the bags. 'What took you so long?'

'It's rush hour,' Veronica pointed out wryly.

'I meant to fly from Auckland,' laughed Karen. 'You should have come via Los Angeles, the way we did, instead of making all those stops…no wonder you look like a limp dishrag!'

Veronica immediately felt the savage burden of her twenty-four years.

'It was the best deal I could find,' she said mildly, knowing that her sister would naturally have been flying all-expenses-paid, in business class.

She collapsed on the soft couch in the light and airy living room, and gratefully slipped her shoes off her aching feet as she accepted the offer of a cup of tea.

Karen, of course, was looking as beautiful as ever—her stretchy tube-top and denim miniskirt accentuating her concave belly and long, skinny legs as she chattered around the kitchen. Not having seen her for nearly a year, Veronica wondered when she had become so sophisticated. No one looking at her now would guess she had been born on a farm.

Although they had both grown up to be exactly the same height, curvaceous Veronica had always felt like an ungainly giantess when she stood beside her little sister. Karen's body was wafer-thin, supple and graceful, her flawless skin without a single, disfiguring freckle, her artfully streaked hair falling halfway down her back in a smooth and shining blonde waterfall. Her long, oval face could have come straight from a painting by Modigliani, her fly-away eyebrows and high cheekbones giving her a haughty look, which dissolved into elfin mischief when she smiled.

People were willing to forgive her a lot to be on the receiving end of that smile. It was no wonder she had lived something of a charmed life, and had consequently ended up a little spoiled and thoughtless.

How thoughtless Veronica discovered a little later, when, the welcoming flurry of greetings and family news dispensed with, Karen admitted the reason for her non-appearance at the airport.

She was busy packing, all right, just not for France!

'The *Caribbean*?' Veronica was thunderstruck. 'Leaving on *Sunday*?' she repeated dumbly. 'B-but—that's the day before we go to Paris!'

Karen flipped her hair back over her shoulders, her brilliant smile a mixture of defiant excitement and shamefaced guilt. She pressed her manicured, be-ringed hands together in an exaggerated *mea culpa*.

'I know! I should have told you about it, but it was only confirmed in the last few days, and you had already prepaid for everything by then and were practically on your way…but, oh, Ronnie, isn't it fantastic?' she gushed, as if her sheer enthusiasm could roll back her sister's bewildered shock.

'I…didn't even know that you were interested in modelling,' Veronica said hollowly. She felt physically sick with disappointment, the light-headedness that had dogged her since her flight increasing exponentially, until she felt as if her head were a hot-air balloon, floating off her shoulders.

Karen was gabbling now: 'I met someone who said I should give it a go, so I had my portfolio done in Auckland and I've been taking it around the agencies here on my days off. I even managed to get a couple of little jobs—just a few hours each. Do you *know* how hard it is to get a break into the modelling scene in London? Especially the fashion side of things—so this is, like, a chance in a *zillion*! Ronnie, *it's a week in the Bahamas* for a series of fashion spreads, not just once in one magazine! I'm substituting for a girl who broke the terms of her contract by putting on too much weight—which I guess makes it *my* big, fat break,' she joked with artless cruelty, skipping swiftly on when she saw it didn't raise a smile.

'The agent said that the *clients* said that if they'd seen my portfolio before, they would have picked *me* over the original girl in the first place. They wanted an unknown for a totally new look and I'm it!' She ran her hands down over her hips in a self-consciously preening gesture, which Veronica watched with dazed grey eyes.

'But you already have a job,' she murmured blankly.

Since she was seventeen, her sister had worked for internationally successful New Zealand food author, Melanie Reed, first as a child-minder, then full-time nanny to her youngest daughter—graduating to live-in personal assistant when nine-year-old Sophie had gone off to boarding school. Melanie and her husband had a lavish home-base in Auckland, but, to Veronica's great envy, Karen had travelled extensively with her employer, and for the last two months had been staying in London while Melanie had been working on a new book deal, researching, and taping segments for a television lifestyle programme.

The Reeds had planned a four-week family break in the South of France following Melanie's London engagements, and, when they heard that Veronica was thinking of flying over to holiday with her sister, had offered Karen cheap rent on their Paris apartment and free use of a small lodge in the grounds of their villa in Provence.

'I thought you enjoyed working for Melanie,' Veronica added, thinking of all the other generous perks and privileges that Karen had taken advantage of over the years.

'I did—I do, but it's not what I want to do for the whole rest of my *life*,' Karen declared. 'I mean, I never really *chose* it, did I? It just sort of *happened*. And it's not as if I've got a lot of choices—I'm not clever like you—' the way she tossed off the compliment made it sound almost like an insult '—but, well— *modelling*—I know could do *that*, and it's got to be loads of fun. I might become a famous supermodel and make wads of cash!

'Oh, Ronnie, this is my dream—like, like going to France has always been your dream!' she burst out, seeming not to see the irony in her words. 'I'm not going behind Mel's back, she's totally OK with it—you wouldn't want me to turn down my big chance, would you?' She pinned a mournful expression on her long face as her shoulders slumped.

It was such a patently silly thing to say that Veronica rolled her eyes. Of course she wouldn't selfishly stand in the way of her sister's newly minted ambitions—and Karen knew it!

'Stop looking so tragic,' she ordered, and Karen instantly obeyed, obviously sensing victory in the snappish words.

'Don't be mad at me,' she begged earnestly. 'I know it's incredibly bad timing, but when destiny calls, what can you do?'

Veronica was tempted to roll her eyes again, but controlled herself. Her head had now recovered from its weird floating sensation and had settled to a painful throb.

'You were the one who persuaded me it was such a great idea for us to spend our holiday together—' She sighed, thinking of the whirlwind weeks of excited organising that had followed her late-night phone call to London on her sister's birthday.

'Yes, but you were the one who first brought it up,' Karen pointed out. 'You *wanted* me to persuade you, and once France was mentioned there was no stopping you. You said it would be a great chance for you to pick up some ideas and contacts for your little gift thing.' Her voice became bubbly and teasing again: 'You also had a pret-ty good reason for wanting to be out of New Zealand right now, if I remember rightly—'

'Well, that's all irrelevant now, isn't it?' Veronica cut her off hurriedly. The 'little gift thing' that Karen dismissed so lightly was the new business she was starting up—a corporate and personal gift-buying service, which she was intending to expand from what had been until now a thriving sideline into a fully-fledged company.

She throttled another upsurge of choking disappointment as she faced the full impact of her sister's defection. 'What are we going to do about all our bookings?'

But Karen had it all worked out. She didn't care about losing her half of the expenses—she was going to make all that and more from her modelling, she said. Since everything was prepaid, Veronica should simply stick to the plan—go to Paris for five days, then on down to Provence. When Karen got back from her week or so in the Bahamas, she would get a cheap flight down to Marseilles—and join her sister for the rest of the holiday.

And when Veronica expressed reluctance about imposing herself on the Reeds, Karen scoffed.

'Oh, don't talk rot! They're already down there and expecting you to turn up. It's a self-catering cottage in the garden, not a guest suite in the villa. You've met Melanie and Miles before, and others are just family, so it'll be all very laid-back and casual. Mel likes you, you know she does. She thinks your working for Mum and Dad's organic farm business makes you a kindred spirit. I've been to France before, so it was more for *your* sake than for mine that she made the offer…after I told her all about your secret passion for all things French and how you drooled over her books set there—'

'Oh, you *didn't*?' Veronica groaned, not fooled by her sister's innocent look. Had Melanie recognised the manipulative ploy? 'That just makes it even more awkward—you made me sound as if I was a freeloader, angling for an invite. Maybe I should at least *suggest* some kind of payment—'

'Oh, well,' said Karen meekly, instantly raising Veronica's suspicions. 'I suppose there *is* something you can do that they'd appreciate *much* more than money…'

Melanie, it transpired, had broken her right elbow in a fall on the day of her arrival in Provence, and was going to be wearing a sling for the next four to six weeks. Consequently, she had rung to warn Karen that she might be asked to do a little bit of work during her holiday stay. Of course Karen had agreed, but with her arrival delayed, perhaps Veronica offering her help would be a clever way to repay the Reeds for their generosity without risking offence? Melanie might not take her up on it, after all she had her family there for all her personal needs, including her widowed mother, but if she did require assistance on something relating to her work, it was bound to only be the occasional errand or bit of note-taking—the sort of thing that Veronica could dash off in a jiffy without even breaking a sweat!

Melanie hadn't been the only one who had ended up being manipulated in that little scenario, Veronica thought wryly as she looked out the window at the late-comers to the first-class carriage hurrying to board before the doors began to close.

As for sweating—plenty of that had broken out when what Veronica had dismissed in London as a bad case of jet lag and tried to sleep off with regular doses of paracetamol had been diagnosed as a nasty case of flu by the emergency doctor she had called in a panic when she had staggered into the apartment in rue de Birague with a raging temperature and only a hazy memory of her trip through the Chunnel.

Fortunately the information sheet in the apartment had provided a number that guaranteed a home visit within thirty minutes, but, regretfully, all the sympathetic doctor could do for 'la grippe', he explained in broken English that was far better than her French, was to prescribe double-strength paracetamol to bring down the fever. She had spent two days languishing in her sickbed, alone, miserable, and heartily sorry for herself.

It was no wonder she had gone crazy when she had finally recovered enough to venture out!

She turned her flushed forehead against the cool glass of the window, and when she opened her eyes she saw the last of the stragglers heading towards the front carriages. One of them was a man carrying a laptop, accompanied by a porter wheeling his suitcase on a trolley. Probably heading for one of the other first-class carriages, she deduced with amusement, since everyone else seemed to be carrying all their own luggage.

He was tall, and walked with a loose-limbed stride, which looked lazy, but which had the stout porter trotting to keep up. A white panama hat with a turned-down brim covered most of his head, but it was the short black pony-tail, almost invisible as it tucked down inside the loosely flicked-up collar of his shirt, along with a certain set of his shoulders, that suddenly caught her eye and made her heart jump into her throat.

No. No, it couldn't be!

There were millions of dark-haired men in Paris, and any number of them with hair long enough to be worn in a pony-tail.

She leaned forward, her own pony-tail tickling her collarbone, her gaze fixed on the back of his head, but he continued to look straight ahead, giving her not even a hint of a profile.

Her scrutiny shifted, drifting down over the loose, dark olive shirt hiding the waistband of his straight-legged jeans, to settle on the tight backside encased in the faded denim, throwing a sexy hitch with every striking stride.

It was absurd to think that she recognised it.

She only had a brief moment to judge its familiarity before he suddenly turned and stepped up onto the train. She wrenched her eyes back up to his face just in time to see a hawkish nose and unshaven jaw flash out of sight.

Veronica pushed back in her cushioned seat, sliding her hips forward so that her head sank below the height of the row. She wasn't hiding, just getting comfortable for the trip, she told herself.

Of course it wasn't Lucien. Maybe it was just someone who *looked* a little bit like him, and her guilty imagination had sketched in the rest.

She turned her eyes back to the window as the train slid smoothly out of the station. It was the country she had come to see, and she intended to sit back and enjoy every single moment of her ride to Avignon!

CHAPTER TWO

HER sexy, dark-haired Frenchman was there again.

Veronica knelt on the window-seat and peeped down at the bar across the street, keeping back at the edge of the curtains so that if he glanced up he wouldn't see her face at the open window.

Not that it was likely. He was sitting at his usual table against the wall, just inside the bank of glass doors that had been folded back to open up the quirky little bar to the street, his back to the strip of pavement shaded by the green canvas canopy, his neat pony-tail a glossy black comma on the white collar of his shirt. A half-full glass of beer sat by his hand, and he was dividing his attention between his newspaper and the attractive brunette polishing glasses behind the bar, who was having a lazy disagreement with the *Patron* re-stocking the bottles.

Business was slow, with only one other customer further inside. The bar didn't really hot up until after dark, then it would be jammed with people and throbbing with Latin American music until exactly midnight, when the shutters went up and the patrons were shooed away in a chorus of happy farewells—much to Veronica's relief, for in the narrow rue de Birague the trapped sound was funnelled upwards on the hot air, and she had found that without the windows open the second floor apartment was unbearably hot, especially for someone suffering a 101-degree temperature.

Her first two days in Paris had been an exercise in frustration. Confined to her apartment except for brief, wobbly forays to *la pharmacie* around the corner and the tiny convenience store a few doors up from the bar, Veronica had had little to do but swallow pills, sleep, drink gallons of water, watch the wonderful world of cable television and gaze out her window at her truncated view of Paris.

Her wistful eye had first spied the sexy, dark stranger after she had returned from a cautious, exploratory expedition to test her recovery. He had been sitting at the same table he was at now, lounging sideways in his seat, sipping a bowl of coffee, idly turning the pages of a French newspaper, a pair of wraparound sunglasses dangling from the chest pocket of his polo shirt.

He looked to be somewhere in his late twenties, suntanned, fit and healthy, and she had envied him as she had leaned against the side of the window, gulping down the fruity yoghurt that had been all her stomach could handle for the past few days. As she had brooded on his slashing profile she had also felt a purely feminine tug of attraction, a sexy little tingle that had followed her down for her nap.

She had quickly realised the futility of trying to compress a week's worth of sightseeing into her remaining few days, and had pared down her meticulously planned schedule to simply hit the highlights on her wish-list, but as her appetite and energy had returned in full measure she had ramped up her expectations and thrown herself wholeheartedly into the pursuit of Paris, hungering for more even as she gorged herself on the sights and sensations.

And every time she had passed the bar in rue de Birague, or looked out the apartment window, she couldn't help glancing at a certain table with a little flutter of anticipation.

She hadn't really expected to see him again, but he had been there several times now, usually in the morning, with a coffee, and at various times of the afternoon or early evening with a beer, or glass of wine and a newspaper. She didn't think he was a tourist, she never saw him with a camera, or water-bottle or pocket guidebook—those ubiquitous supplies that every visitor to Paris had grafted to their person—and he seemed to prefer facing away from the street, uninterested in the passing parade. Yet, given the different times of the day she had seen him there, he didn't seem to work, either…at least, not regular hours, anyway. And he was always alone.

Like Veronica…

Her palms dampened as she contemplated what she was about to do.

Bastille Day was her swan-song in Paris and she wanted to see it out in style. Last night she had danced with the thousands at the official party in the Place de la Bastille. This morning she had joined the crowds watching the traditional military parade along the Champs Elysées, and paid her respects at the Tomb of the Unknown Warrior under the Arc de Triomphe. She had lunched in the Latin Quarter and strolled home across the Île de la Cité.

But she had done it all alone, while at every turn she had been confronted by couples of one kind or another…lovers oblivious to those around them, husbands and wives bickering in the blazing heat or strolling hand in hand, parents running after their children, mutual companions sharing a good time…

And now, with late afternoon drifting into evening, she was feeling defiant.

She picked up her bag and checked herself in the mirror one more time, spinning to watch the multi-panelled silk and gauze-chiffon skirt swirl and cling around her long thighs, and adjusting the strap on the filmy black camisole top that daringly showed off the exquisite, embroidered, French lace, strapless bra she wore beneath—all bought in an expensive fit of madness the previous day.

Then, at the last minute, just as she was going out the door, she snatched up a lightweight wrap to throw across her bare shoulders, a security blanket in case her courage failed her.

She walked across the street and straight into the interior of the narrow, rectangular bar, exchanging a casual '*bonjour*' with the pair behind the high, polished counter. The object of her obsession had skewed his seat against the dark-panelled wall and now sat facing out into the room, one elbow on the table, jeaned legs stretched out and crossed at the ankle, so Veronica confidently chose the small table for two diagonally across from him, turning the chair sideways to sit down with her back against the opposing wall.

He took a swallow of his beer, frowning down at his newspaper, seemingly ignoring her when everyone else had turned to watch her settle at her table, but she had seen—and felt—the lightning-swift appraisal he had accorded her when she had crossed the periphery of his field of vision. A woman as tall as she was always attracted at least *one* look.

His eyes were dark. She added that to the list of things she knew about him, her gaze going quickly to his right hand to also tick off the fact that he wore no wedding ring. A little of the nervous tension holding her spine rigid relaxed, and she crossed her legs, slanting them aside in what Karen had informed her during their short time in London together was the most slimming of poses.

When the waitress sauntered over Veronica was ready with her order. She would have actually liked a thirst-quenching beer, but didn't think that that would project the image she was looking to create—although: 'I'm having what he's having,' might have been an ice-breaker. However, at the moment he appeared to be more granite than ice. Whatever he was reading in the paper was putting a scowl on his face. It wasn't *L'Equipe*, which she had seen him reading before, but the French equivalent of scandal-mongering weekly tabloid, so it probably wasn't simply a matter of his favourite tennis player being knocked out of a tournament.

'*Un Kir, s'il vous plaît,*' she murmured to the waitress.

The chilled glass was placed before her a few minutes later accompanied by a friendly burst of rapid French. Veronica spread her hands, palm up, with a rueful smile.

'*Excusez-moi, mais je ne comprends pas,*' she said carefully, in her phrase-book French.

'*Ah! Anglaise,*' the girl instantly pounced on her accent.

Veronica shook her head, setting fiery sparks dancing in the graduated layers of red-brown hair falling thickly down to her shoulders on either side of her central parting.

'*Nouvelle Zélande,*' she said, hoping a European might find that exotic, since in the intimate confines of the small premises the man across the way would be able to hear every word she said, even if he was ostensibly not listening.

Veronica took a delicate sip of her drink, enjoying the crispness of the white wine mingled with the sweet tang of crème de cassis. She looked brazenly at her quarry.

At close range his face was a series of bold lines, his sun-kissed olive skin fine-textured and smooth except for the bloom of dark re-growth along his jaw. His arched black brows were lowered, sensuous lower lip pushed out as he brooded into the dregs of his beer.

Eyes fixed on his face, she took another hasty sip of liquid courage, and the stem of her glass clicked loudly as she put it down a little too hard on the table.

His long, thick lashes flew up and she suddenly found herself pinned by a fierce black look. Even if he had been studiously ignoring her he had obviously been aware of her concentrated stare.

She didn't make the mistake of smiling. She sensed that was what he was expecting her to do, and didn't want to give him the opportunity to snub her even before she had got to open her mouth, so instead she simply held his gaze coolly, her wide grey eyes drifting slightly out of focus as if she weren't really seeing him at all, but absently thinking of something—or someone—else.

She might not be very experienced at seduction—her ex-fiancé had been very conservative in the bedroom—or have the advantage of her sister's spectacular beauty, but she was intelligent and well-read, and she knew that there were more subtle ways to tease a man's interest. Some of the most famous, and infamous, seductresses in history had been women who had more wit than beauty. Attraction started in the brain, after all.

She saw his eyelids flicker and his lower lip tighten. Her lack of reaction had disconcerted him, disclosing a dichotomy in his nature. He might not want attention, but neither did he like to be ignored, she decided. He was used to it being *his* choice as to whether or not he interacted with people.

He leaned back in his chair, picking up one foot to rest the heel of his high-end athletic shoe on his opposing knee, his pre-stressed designer jeans whitening along the seams at his crotch, his thighs splayed towards her in a stark display of male insolence.

Was he partially aroused already, or just more generously endowed than the classical male? she wondered naughtily, mentally comparing him to all the nude statuary she had perused in the last few days.

Now she allowed herself a small, reminiscent smile as she toyed with her drink, her pale fingers sliding delicately up and down on the long stem of the glass.

He picked up his paper from the table and snapped it open in front of his face with a sharp rattle, but Veronica noticed with a small sizzle of satisfaction that he was holding the top of it just below the level of his eyes. He was covertly observing her, just as she was studying him.

Her lashes lowered, and she saw a tiny teardrop of condensation weeping down the outside of the curved bowl of her glass. Acting on a primitive instinct, she chased it back up to the rim with her forefinger, lifting the captured little pearl of liquid away on the tip of her finger and inspecting it before placing it inside her mouth and sucking off the distilled droplet. She noticed the side of the newspaper crinkle under his tightened grip, and, alarmed by her own boldness, she polished off the rest of her drink in a single toss of her head and ordered a second Kir.

Almost immediately, *he* signalled for another beer.

Veronica almost fainted with nervous relief. He wasn't just going to get up and leave! Although at this rate they were going to drink each other under the table before they said a word to each other, she thought with an inward gurgle of amusement.

For a while she was content to sit and bide her time, listening and occasionally being drawn in by the general comments about the heatwave and the state of the city that the *Patron* periodically offered around the bar—in heavily accented English to Veronica, Spanish to the waitress and French to the man barely pretending to read his newspaper, who replied with concise, but perfectly amiable comments in both of the Romance languages.

How appropriate…the whispered thought brought a husky laugh to Veronica's lips, the unusually deep voice, which had often embarrassed her as a teenager, suddenly an advantage as it drew dark eyes snapping to her face.

This time she was ready for him. She let her laugh die to a natural throaty chuckle as she held his gaze, picked up her drink, and walked the three steps to his table.

'*Parlez-vous Anglais?*' she asked, her resonant voice warm with the remnants of laughter.

He tilted his head back to look up at her and folded his arms across his chest, the open paper lying forgotten across his splayed knees.

'*Non!*' The uncompromisingly curt answer was delivered like a flung gauntlet.

His eyes weren't black, as she had first thought, but brown, like the darkest of dark chocolate, the best and most expensive kind…intense, slightly bitter at first but delivering the most delicious sensory thrill.

At the moment they were veiled and enigmatic, not giving a hint as to his thoughts as he waited to see how she would handle the flat rejection.

'Oh.' She sank into the chair on the other side of his narrow table. *'Je ne parle pas bien française.'*

Her trusty little French phrase book was tucked in her purse, but tonight wasn't a night for going by the book.

He shrugged, pushing out that sullen lower lip to indicate his unspoken contempt. Trying to look unruffled, she took a leisurely sip of her drink. She knew he spoke some Spanish, but that was no help as far as she was concerned.

'Italiano?' she tested, although she only spoke a basic word or two herself.

His stony expression didn't change. *'Non.'*

'Hmm…' She eyed the angle of his chin, and understood that he was going to stick stubbornly to French, whatever she said. But she could be stubborn, too. It was one of her greatest strengths…and her biggest flaw, according to Neil, her ex-fiancé.

'Te reo Maori?' she threw in mischievously, seriously doubting that he would be of the minority speakers of New Zealand's second language, especially when he didn't even speak the first—English.

Or did he?

She detected a dark glimmer in the back of the brown eyes as his mouth compressed. Was that a tiny quiver of amusement at the down-turned corner? She felt a surge of elation.

She decided to let go of her security blanket and allowed her wrap to slide from her shoulders, turning to drape it across the back of her chair, her twisting movements drawing attention to the whiteness of her lightly freckled shoulders against the blackness of the chiffon top.

As she turned back she almost blushed to feel the nervous rise and fall of her breasts, cupped in their luxuriant nests of embroidered tulle, against the sheer silk. Every breath felt like a wanton act of provocation.

And naturally he looked…he *was* a man, after all…with a thoughtful expression that was somehow more stimulating than a leer, and Veronica was thankful for the strategic pleats of tulle when she felt the tips of her breasts begin to tingle and harden into betraying little points.

'Russian? Icelandic?' A slight breathlessness made her voice even more husky as she resumed their game.

His gaze fell back to his newspaper and for a shattering moment she feared that she had overplayed her hand. She looked around for inspiration, glancing over at the owner of the bar, who had been following the progress of their encounter with frank interest. To her chagrin he grinned and gave an expressive shrug, as if to indicate the hopelessness of her case.

'*Sprechen Sie Deutsches?*'

Veronica's head whipped back to find the chocolate-brown eyes waiting for her, banked with a taunting amusement, the roughly folded newspaper wedged down the side of the table.

The wretch!

'*Nein,*' she said, giving him look for look. '*Je parle anglais seulement,*' she stressed, admitting her language deficiency with a defiant tilt of her chin.

A slow, sexy smile trawled across his mouth.

'*Je suis désolé,*' he said, placing a mocking hand across his heart.

She understood *that*, but chose to turn his mockery back on him: '*Et je suis Veronica,*' she replied pertly.

He laughed and inclined his head. 'Lucien.'

Effervescent emotion bubbled up inside her. She offered him her hand across the table. 'Pleased to meet you, Lucien.'

'Enchanté,' he murmured, and she shivered as she felt the warm slide of his palm against hers, his thumb caressing up over her knuckles, his breath warm on the back of her hand as he lifted it to his mouth, holding her gaze as his lips brushed lightly over her skin.

It was a ridiculously over-extravagant cliché of a gesture, as they both well knew, but it still made Veronica feel hot all over, and when she disengaged her hand she wrapped it quickly around her glass in a vain attempt to cool off.

Noticing that his beer-glass was almost empty, she tried to buy some more time by ordering another round, but he protested when she tried to get herself another Kir and she became even more flushed at the idea that he thought she was drunk. But no—by word, gesture and helpful translation from the bar-owner, she divined that he was changing her order to a Kir Royale, and putting it on his own bill.

It was, she discovered, made with champagne rather than still white wine, and was an altogether more superior drink. Judging from her peep of the Champagne label on the bottle that the barman had discreetly turned away to pour, it was also a great deal more superior in price. Her dark-haired companion, then, was obviously not a poor man…something she had already deduced from the expensive labels on his casual clothes.

The champagne went immediately to her head, and banished her former nerves and with them any remaining doubts about the wisdom of what she was doing. You didn't need to speak the same language, she discovered, in order to have a good time—in fact, in some ways it was more liberating *not* to have to make sense!

The language differences made deep conversation impossible, but neither of them was in a mood to be serious, so over the course of the evening they invented their own way of com-

municating. Across the twin barriers of language and a mutual
reluctance to touch on personal subjects, they established the
important basics: the fact they were both single, over twenty-
one, and currently alone in Paris—she in need of a knowl-
edgeable guide to the best places to be in Paris on Bastille
Night, and he…well…her feeble French wasn't up to ques-
tioning his motives even if she had wanted to. It was enough
that he found her an entertaining diversion from whatever it
was that had had him brooding darkly over his newspaper.

When her stomach gurgled an embarrassing message, he
paid their shot at the bar and whisked her around a few corners
to the Brasserie Bofinger, where they sat on plush banquettes
under the spectacular art nouveau glass dome, and gorged
themselves on oysters and champagne. He was amused at
their pantomimed tussle over the bill and sulked at her iron-
willed insistence on paying it with her credit card, but, catching the devilish gleam in his eye, she suspected he was putting
on a great deal of his outrage, and that he enjoyed messing
with her head, much as she had enjoyed toying with his expectations, playing to the hilt his role of volatile and moody,
but ultimately charming, Frenchman.

At times during the rest of the magical night she had reason
to suspect that he might not even be French, and that he definitely understood more English than he was letting on—but
neither mattered, for the mystery was all part of the fun.

All that mattered was that he knew Paris—inventive
enough to slip them past hotel security for a peek at a glittering masquerade ball and persuasive enough to talk them into
the exclusive nightclub of her fancy.

He was also strong enough to muscle their way through the
crowds and quick-thinking enough to rescue them when they
emerged from the Métro at the Bastille, where they had agreed
to say their farewells, to be caught up in a furious scuffle between a flying wedge of riot police and a rowdy mob of po-

litical protesters intermingled with drunken youths looking to encourage the fight.

'Luc!' she cried as she received a stray elbow in the kidney that almost knocked her to the ground.

'This way!' Lucien yelled in her ear, hooking his powerful arm around Veronica's waist, swinging her away from the moving wall of riot shields and flailing batons, and ducking and diving with her amongst the fleeing crowds being herded away from the centre of the action.

Cutting left down the rue de la Bastille with several dozen others, they ran past the familiar long red awning of Bofinger and right at the next corner, Lucien's arm falling away to grab her hand, and Veronica blindly trusted herself to his lead, breathlessly running helter-skelter in her flimsy sandals at his side, past the rows of parked cars, and tooting traffic, quickly outstripping the other scattering runners who slowed when the police turned their attention to easier prey. She began to laugh helplessly, for the sheer absurdity of it: Veronica Bell, budding businesswoman and long time goody-two-shoes, on the run from the cops through the night streets of Paris!

They cut left again, and suddenly they were in a place she recognised—the open-sided pedestrian arcade surrounding the Place des Vosges, their running footsteps on the stone paving echoing off the vaulted ceiling. Lights were on in some of the apartments in the seventeenth-century, red-brick buildings facing out onto the square, but the restaurants and cafés and art galleries in the arcade below were closed. Here the shouting and the tumult seemed a long way away, little traffic turning through the square, the park gates locked and the fountains turned off, the neatly clipped row of linden trees around the edge of the park casting ghostly shadows onto the crushed white walkways inside the iron railings.

'You spoke English,' Veronica accused, tugging at his hand

as she slowed down, her chest burning, her free hand pressing against the slight stitch in her side.

She gasped as a police car slid past the end of the square and Lucien spun her behind one of the square pillars that supported the arched ceiling of the arcade, backing her up against the cool stone, his hands sliding around her back to protect her silk top from the roughened surface as his body pressed her deep into the inky shadow. Their panting breath intermingled and she could feel the rapid beat of his heart kicking against her breast and the fear and excitement tangled up inside her until she had to struggle to think.

'Back there,' she whispered hoarsely, 'I heard you—'

He muttered something that could have been French or English or any language under the sun, because by then he was kissing her and nothing mattered any more but the intoxicating taste of his mouth, the spicy scent of his skin filling her nostrils and the feel of his arms tightening around her, crushing her soft breasts against his hard chest. The brush with danger had been arousing and now there was another way to feed their inflamed emotions and ramp up the heart-tingling excitement. Adrenalin spiked in her veins as Lucien bit her tender lip and forced his way into her mouth, his tongue spearing hotly into the silky depths as his hips ground into hers, flattening her bottom against the cool stone. It was pure, plundering, passionate savagery—nothing, *nothing*, like the light, teasing kisses he had given her earlier at the fireworks…nothing like any kiss she had ever had before in her life!

Veronica hadn't known what she was missing, but she did now, her inhibitions swept away by his maddening skill. Surrounded by his embrace, her arms trapped at her sides, her hands could only grip at his flanks, her fingers curving under the rise of his buttocks, her short nails digging demandingly into the tight denim weave as she squirmed against him, causing him to shudder and groan her name, plunging deeper into her mouth. The sound of other voices echoing within the arcade wrenched them back into an awareness of their surroundings, but only long enough to acknowledge the raw urgency of their desire.

'Come…' was all he said, in a smouldering voice, thick with promise, and she would have followed him to the moon. But heaven wasn't even further than the next street. He kissed her from pillar to pillar, all the way along the arcade, and once out into rue de Birague he managed the pretence of control just long enough to get her into his apartment, Veronica hugging her delicious secret as they passed her door on the way up the stairs.

She had never thought of herself as wildly sexy until she saw herself through Lucien's eyes. He wanted her and wasn't afraid to let her see it, made demands of her that unlocked the secret desires that she didn't even know that she possessed. And never had a man undressed for her the way he did… slowly, sensuously stripping off his clothes without taking his eyes off her face, watching her watch him reveal his body's flagrant readiness for love-making, seeing the hectic flush of passion turn her pale, freckle-flecked skin to rose-pink, her grey eyes widen then darken in a shocked fascination that revealed more than she knew, her kiss-swollen mouth parting in luscious anticipation of tasting his tawny flesh, her awed appreciation when he prowled naked towards her making him chuckle, his healthy male ego basking in the flattery.

And then it was her turn, the sultry stroke of his admiring gaze appeasing her shyness, telling her without words how magnificent he found the lavish proportions of her tall body as he unzipped her skirt and let it fall to the floor, tantalisingly delaying the thrilling moment when he slid his palms under her silk camisole, skimming her swollen breasts in the sexy lingerie as he raked it up over her head, bending his worshipful mouth to the lush, creamy slopes bared by the scalloped lace edge of the lavender bra. His hands were as skilful and busy as his mouth and Veronica closed her eyes as sheer, unadulterated, sensual bliss began to roll over her in waves…

One of which dashed cold water in her face!

Veronica's eyes flew open, her flush of arousal turning into an embarrassed blush as she registered the gentle rock of the TGV, and realised that a little girl in a pink dress had tripped on her unsteady progress up the aisle and splattered her with chilled water from the open bottle in her hand. Avoiding her innocent young face, Veronica hoped that her X-rated memories weren't emblazoned on her pink forehead as she accepted the scrambling apologies from the girl's American mother, assuring her with a cheerful smile that mineral water was excellent for the complexion.

She patted the water into her hot skin as they continued on their progress, chagrined to realise that she had nodded off— although that wasn't surprising in view of her lack of sleep— and had been reliving her intensely erotic encounter in vivid Technicolor instead of paying attention to the fascinating parade of French towns and villages popping up into sight as the train whipped past the rolling fields of the French countryside.

And now it was too late. According to the multilingual announcement broadcast through the carriage, the high-speed train was slowing down on the approach to the outskirts of Avignon. She would have to make certain she paid attention on the return trip, Veronica lectured herself.

Someone had discarded a newspaper on the floor beside Karen's empty seat and she automatically leaned over to pick it up, grimacing as she noticed that it was the same one that Lucien had been reading in the bar. She idly flicked through it, only able to pick out a few words and phrases here and there. Much of the centre of the paper was illustrated with typical paparazzi shots of the usual set of international celebrities caught in embarrassing situations, and Veronica skipped over them, uninterested in the misdoings of minor royals and rock stars going into rehab, or the big *Exclusivité*—a string of photos of a notoriously volatile actor having some kind of punch-up in a London hotel. On impulse she tucked it into her bag. She would throw it away later, she promised herself— she didn't need any proxy souvenirs of her night on the town!

As she manhandled her case down the long flight of concrete stairs to the group of glass boxes housing the rental car agencies outside the Avignon TGV station, Veronica was glad that she had had the forethought to buy herself a wide-brimmed straw hat at a Paris market. The heatwave that was baking Paris had also tightened its relentless grip on the South of France, and the aching blue sky was adazzle, the temperature already in the mid-thirties, even though the sun wasn't yet at its height.

There was a long queue for the rental car, but it moved surprisingly quickly and she was soon stepping back out into the blazing sun nervously clutching the key to her VW Golf. Setting out for the car park, she glanced over towards the adjacent rental agencies and stopped dead, oblivious to the flow of people around her, as she saw a man leaning against one of the counters, laptop and suitcase at his feet, panama hat in hand, joking with the girl handing him a sheet of paper.

It *was* Luc! The man in the olive shirt and jeans from the Gare de Lyon… Absolutely, unmistakably him!

Snapped out of her stunned trance by a cranky, sunburnt tourist trying to get his suitcase between a concrete bollard and her stalled luggage, Veronica hurried on her way, her thoughts whirling.

Surely this was one spooky coincidence too many, she thought as she quickly shovelled her possessions into the boot of her shiny blue compact and got behind the wheel.

Had he followed her? She remembered telling him at some stage that she would be spending most of her holiday in the

South of France, although she hadn't specified when or how she was leaving. At the time he had gone into a long, and hilariously incomprehensible, rhapsody about the Côte d'Azur, and from the questions she had tried to ask about the famous beaches there he might have thought that was where she was headed.

If he had been talking about his *own* imminent plans to travel down to the Mediterranean coast then perhaps this *could* just be shrugged off as another of life's little strange twists. At the time, it might have amused him to think that they could conceivably run into each other on a beach in Nice or Cannes.

Her pleasure in the thought curdled as her imagination continued to flourish. But what if he *had* somehow managed to track her down for some sinister purpose of his own? What if he was a *stalker*? she fretted. Or some kind of conman or kinky killer whom she had thwarted by sneaking off before he could achieve his evil aims?

She suddenly laughed at her wild speculations. In reality, she and Lucien had been ships passing in the night, and all either of them had expected to carry away from their brief encounter was the memory of a good time!

There was a perfectly innocent explanation for them to be crossing paths again. Luc had been carrying a laptop, so perhaps he had come down to Avignon on business. He was probably self-employed, like Veronica, and could pick and choose his working hours.

She was nervous enough about driving on the right-hand side of the road for the first time, as well as doing her own navigation, without adding the paranoic fear that she was being trailed by a psychotic serial killer!

CHAPTER THREE

VERONICA sighed with contentment as she sat at her table under a spreading plane tree in the tiny village square and sipped her cup of coffee, enjoying the faint breeze that feathered warmly around her bare neck and riffled the end of her pony-tail.

Karen had said the Reeds wouldn't expect her to arrive at their villa, Mas de Bonnard, on the outskirts of the little village of St Romain-de-Vaucluse, until mid-afternoon. As a direct drive, it was only about forty minutes north-east of Avignon, so she had decided to take it slowly, avoiding the larger roads and towns and following the meandering scenic route that Melanie had recommended as being the one they preferred as the prettiest. She had even suggested this very café as worthy of a stop.

Veronica cut another sliver from her glistening pastry and popped it into her mouth, savouring the intense burst of apricot on her tongue.

A sleek silver convertible with red upholstery slid into the cobbled square, following the lone street that passed through the village. As it drew level and slowed almost to a stop for a scamper of children chasing a small dog, the driver lazily took a survey of his surroundings. His eyes were masked by wrap-around sunglasses, but Veronica saw his glossy black head jerk in a rapid double take. His jaw visibly dropped, then tightened with a snap and the car braked to an abrupt halt. A long arm was slung across the top of the empty passenger seat as the driver twisted to look over his shoulder and backed sharply in to park parallel with the kerb, springing out of the car without bothering to open the door.

In a few ground-eating strides he was standing in front of her, his black shadow stamping his presence on the sun-dappled tablecloth.

'Well, isn't this a cosy little reunion!'

Coffee slopped into her saucer as she flinched at the sarcastic drawl. She looked up into Lucien's blazing brown eyes, his wraparound sunglasses pushed up on top of his head unmasking his hard expression, his hands planted on his hips, legs astride, male aggression oozing from every gorgeous pore.

Her brain went into panic mode as every female cell in her body rioted with delight at his proximity.

'What are you doing here? Are you following me?' she blurted, half in hope, half in horror.

There was a brief pause, as if he was taken aback by the response. The shock on his face when he had seen her from the car had been completely spontaneous, she acknowledged wretchedly, her hands clenching as she fought to control her humiliation.

'Are you going to stab me with that if I don't give you the answer you want?' he asked warily, and she lowered her eyes to see that she was gripping the knife she had used to cut her pastry, holding it defensively in front of her body. She hastily let it clatter back onto the plate. She could always scream if he tried anything violent. They were in a public place, after all.

Unlike last night.

The last time she had spoken to this man they had both been naked in his bed, making hot, passionate love!

She blushed, and the predatory light that had been banked in his eyes flared into renewed life.

He hooked out a chair from the adjacent table with a swipe of his foot and spun it around to sit astride, folding his arms along the top. Through the thin vertical slats of the back of the chair she could see that the sides of his olive shirt hung open revealing a white singlet, the circular discs of his flat brown nipples clearly visible against the thin fabric.

'Lost for words, Veronica?' he asked with an insolent smile. 'You had plenty to say last night…*c'est vrai*?'

The taunt jerked her flustered eyes back to his expectant face as recognition of his true perfidiousness hit her like a blow.

'And you're very fluent in English all of a sudden,' she said acidly. 'You don't even appear to have any accent.'

'I'm a certified genius,' was his sardonic reply. 'I learn fast.' From his taunting grin she knew he didn't expect her to believe him, his teeth lethally white against his tan. He spoke English like a native—a man who was aware of every subtlety and nuance of the language.

'You're no more French than I am!' she spluttered, desperately trying to remember what betraying words she might have whispered to him in the throes of ecstasy, secure in the knowledge that he wouldn't understand a word.

'I never said I was.' He shrugged.

'You never said you weren't, either,' she said bitterly.

His mouth twisted. 'I thought that was the deal: don't ask, don't tell…because you certainly made no attempt to question who or what I was. But now I think it's because you already *knew* who I was before you even walked into that bar. That was no chance meeting between us, was it, Veronica?'

Her grey eyes slid evasively away from his darkly accusing gaze as she remembered spying on him from her apartment window.

'It wasn't like that—'

'Oh, what *was* it like?' he pressed.

She shuddered at the thought of trying to explain, and attempted to fall back on her simmering grievance. 'There was no need for you to pretend you didn't speak a word of English,' she said weakly.

'Like you claimed you didn't understand French,' he shot back.

She blinked. 'That's because I *don't*—'

'Then how do you explain your choice of reading material?' He bent over and plucked out the tabloid newspaper sticking up from her canvas carry-bag, which was leaning against the leg of the table by her sandalled feet. 'Or are you going to claim you just bought it for the pretty pictures?' he added with a sneering emphasis.

'I haven't read it—it's not mine,' she said quickly, unwilling to admit to the foolish impulse that made her pick it up— the desire for some sort of continuing connection with him, however tenuous. 'Someone left it on the train,' she muttered. 'I meant to throw it away, I just forgot about it...'

'That's convenient—there's a rubbish bin over there by the corner,' he pointed out. 'I'll dump it in there right now, shall I, and save you the bother of doing it later?' And under her startled gaze he jumped up and suited his actions to his words, stuffing the paper well down into the depths of the bin, and walking back towards her, dusting off his hands with an air of grim satisfaction.

He had just made certain that whatever in the paper that he so savagely objected to was now beyond the means of her finding out, she realised, watching him in wide-eyed wariness as he straddled his chair again, waving away the waiter who approached to ask for his order.

He rested his darkly stubbled chin on his folded arms. 'Now, what were we talking about? Oh, yes, our mutual charade last night. Did you rifle through my things, by the way, before you left?'

She stiffened. 'Why would I? I'm not a thief!'

He straightened, shedding his air of mocking insolence. 'What else was I supposed to think when I woke up to find you'd done a moonlight flit? And here I thought that Kiwis were a flightless bird.'

'It was morning—there wasn't any moon.' She wasn't going to tell him that it was inexperience and embarrassment that had caused her to panic. 'I—I had things to do.'

'And people to call?' he suggested. He tilted his head, a shaft of sunlight through the branches of the plane tree turning his eyes to polished bronze.

'One or two,' she admitted, puzzled by his sudden tension. She had rung her parents for a quick check-in before the next leg of her trip, carefully avoiding any mention of illness, and had texted her sister without much hope of an informative reply.

'Including your employer, perhaps?' Lucien murmured, to her added bewilderment. 'In London…?'

Veronica's dark brown eyebrows snapped together. 'I don't have one as such; I'm self-employed. And I told you, I'm from New Zealand—'

'You're freelance?' he cut her off, with a disparaging look down his hawkish nose that raised her hackles.

'I prefer to call myself an independent businesswoman,' she told him.

His face hardened. 'Well, whatever you call yourself, my advice is to stop throwing yourself into my path because I don't like being harassed, and French privacy laws happen to be quite strict in that respect. You might find yourself being tossed out of the country on your plush white bottom. I think your opening line in this conversation was rather ironic considering the way you've been carrying on!'

Her mouth fell open. 'You think *I'm* following *you*?' she said, her deep voice rich with scorn. She started to laugh, then stopped when she realised from his tight-lipped expression that he was actually serious. 'That's crazy! How on earth could I have followed you, when *I* was the one who got here first?' she pointed out triumphantly.

'Only because I had one or two things to pick up in Avignon before I left,' he countered. 'Did you think I didn't notice you lurking around while I was renting my car? What did you do? Go back and bribe the girl on the desk to tell you where I said I was going so you could take the same road?'

Veronica gasped. 'I wasn't *lurking*,' she said. 'I was picking up my own rental. I didn't even realise you'd seen me,' she added stiffly, not realising it could be interpreted as a guilty admission.

'Oh, come on. There aren't that many towering redheads around that you didn't stand out like a beacon—'

'Then I obviously wasn't lurking, was I?' she snapped. 'And my hair isn't red.' Being a strapping, six-foot tall female had made the teasing bad enough at high school, without accepting the added stigma of being a 'ginger'.

His eyes followed the movement. 'It certainly burns bright under the Provence sun. Why do you think all those famous painters came down here to produce their masterpieces? Because of the special quality of the light, and the way it affects the human perception of colour.'

'Is that why you've come here? You're a painter?' she said. A volatile artistic temperament might go a long way to explaining, if not excusing, his behaviour. Maybe that tabloid he had been so furious about had given a rotten review of his work.

He stood up. 'Nice try, Veronica,' he said cynically. 'Those big, bemused eyes are a convincing touch, but it's a little late to feign innocence.'

He bent, angling his torso across the narrow table and bracing his hands flat on the crumb-strewn cloth on either side of her unconsciously bunched fists, and thrusting his face close enough for her to feel the heat of his menacing purr.

'This is your first and last warning, Veronica—stay well away from me and everything that's mine or I'll make you rue the day you ever came to France.' He jerked slightly, as if to leave, but then settled back, one hand moving up to cup her jaw, firmly tilting her pale, freckled face to his. 'And by the way, just off the record, between the two of us—' he rocked forward on his toes and kissed her square on her stunned mouth, taking his own, sweet time over it before he pulled back to conclude '—thanks for the memories. You were great last night, a real handful in more ways than one—the best lay I've had in a long, long time…'

And he walked down to the kerb, jumped into his car and was gone in a rumbling roar of exhaust fumes before she could recover sufficiently to throw her empty coffee-cup at his arrogant head. Her hand went to her bare throat and she realised that in the turmoil of their exchange she had never thought to ask about her pendant. Perhaps she should have accused *him* of being the thief!

Hours later as Veronica did another careful circuit of the narrow roads on the outskirts of St Romain-de-Vaucluse she was still festering over his insolence and inventing the clever comebacks that had escaped her at the time.

Thanks for the memories? The *best lay.* They ranked alongside the 'plush bottom' remark for sheer, face-slapping gall.

If she ever saw him again, she decided, she *would* slap his face.

She lifted her foot off the accelerator, slowing down as she approached the intersection of two roads leading out of the village in different directions where, according to Karen's roughly sketched map, Mas de Bonnard was supposedly located.

She recognised the main route by which she had first entered the village and, not wanting to go further out in the wrong direction, she did a U-turn, and came back to park on a rough grass verge beside a large, open acreage of vines stretching away in parallel rows from the roadside with nary a sign of a fence or hedge marking out the edges of the property, very unlike the farms and vineyards of home. She sighed and rested her elbow on the open driver's window while she sipped at her lukewarm bottle of water, looking towards the church steeple and clock-tower she could see rising above the tops of the venerable plane trees that lined the narrow main street, and had made it such a challenge for her to negotiate. It seemed to still be siesta-time, for there were few people moving about. Heat lay like a blanket over the countryside, the cream and brown houses of plaster and stone in the historic village looking as if they had grown up out of the rocky land itself. It was an idyllic scene, incredibly peaceful—if you discounted the ceaseless chorus of the cicadas, loudly quacking away in the trees like a flock of miniature ducks.

As if to contradict her, the bell-tower chimed the half-hour and two teenagers on motor scooters buzzed past the corner shouting catcalls to each other.

Maybe if she made the five-minute drive around the village one more time she might be able to better orientate herself to the wiggly lines on the map. Or she could buy herself something at one of the little shops or cafés in the main street and lower herself to actually ask for directions. She wasn't really in any hurry, so it didn't matter if she took all afternoon to trace her hosts.

She heard a metal creak and turned to see a man coming out of a large, barred double-gate in the high stone wall on the other side of the tar-sealed road.

'Are you just browsing around the area, or looking to buy that particular vineyard?' he inquired with a smile as he sauntered up to her open window.

Veronica smiled back. 'I wish! Just browsing, thanks, Miles—and sitting here trying to make head or tail of this map of Karen's! I didn't realise I was right on top of you.'

Miles Reed's weathered face creased in a chuckle. 'Hello,

Veronica. We weren't sure it was you at first. We watched you whiz past a few times before Melanie thought she recognised that reddish hair—'

He didn't notice her flinch as he continued, 'Don't blame your sister—everyone gets confused. The roads are very wiggly-waggly around here. If you turn around, I'll open up the gates for you. Bear left when you come in and you'll see the parking bay where you can leave your car.'

The paved driveway sloped gently down and curved around a profusion of tall, flowering shrubs and clusters of cherry, apricot and almond trees before splitting into two—one broad section turning right towards the large, two-storeyed stone house overlooking a cobbled courtyard and the other, narrower drive terminating in a vine-covered pergola next to the windowless back wall of a small, rectangular cottage with rough-plastered walls painted the colour of clotted cream and deep-set windows covered by blue shutters.

Miles followed her down on foot and handed her two keys on a small ring. 'One for the gate, one for the cottage,' he told her as she opened the boot of her car. 'Let me help you take these bags around—Melanie should be along in a minute to show you all you need to know about the cottage. She was just trying to drag Sophie out of the pool.

'I hope you had a good trip from Paris,' he said, swinging out her larger case as if it weighed no more than a feather and reaching in for the soft roll-bag. For a man in his early sixties he had the vigour and energy of a much younger man, perhaps because of his very physical lifestyle, being very much of a hands-on builder, according to Karen. 'And you found your way to St Romain with no nasty little surprises on the road from Avignon.'

Just one big one! Veronica bent over to refasten the buckle on the side of her case and when she straightened her face was excusably pink.

'It was a very interesting drive,' she admitted with perfect truth.

She followed Miles down the steps and around onto a sunny, paved patio edged with flowering plants at the front of the cottage, where he put down her bags beside a wrought-iron table and chairs.

'I'm very grateful to you both for allowing me to stay,' she added shyly, looking around the walled garden with its wonderful profusion of plants and trees, a white, crushed-stone pathway leading off between two stone pillars to join the sweeping curve of the main driveway. Only just, through the tracery of leaves and branches, could she make out an occasional glimpse of the clay-tiled roof of the main house.

Miles ran his stubby, carpenter's fingers through his healthy thatch of iron-grey hair. 'We're the ones who're grateful, Veronica. After all, your holiday is just as important as ours.'

'Uh, yes, well…thank you,' murmured Veronica, not quite sure what he meant. 'I was sorry to hear about Melanie's accident…'

'Aren't we all!' he said, pulling a face. 'It threw a real spanner in the works. She's been planning this big get-together for so long she was furious at being told she'd have to curtail her activities and wear a sling—particularly the bit about not being able to drive!'

Big get-together? Veronica felt a ripple of dismay. 'How many are coming? I was sure that Karen said it was only going to be your family…'

'Oh, I didn't mean big in terms of numbers, there's only seven of us,' he explained, to her relief, 'but the kids are so rarely all in the same place at the same time any more, that it's a Very Big Deal for Melanie, especially since it was planned around her mother's seventy-fifth birthday…' He gave her a long-suffering roll of his hazel eyes. 'No family holiday is complete without the old ma-in-law tagging along, right?'

Veronica laughed, because she had seen them together, and knew that he and Zoe Main got on extremely well. She also knew that two of their three offspring were no longer 'kids' in the strict sense of the word. The twenty-one-year-old twins might object to being put in the same grade as their much younger sister.

'And, of course, Melanie's stepson from her first marriage has agreed to come too, so that makes it even more of a VBD as far as she's concerned,' Miles said.

'Oh, I didn't even know she'd been married before,' she murmured in surprise.

'Long ago and very briefly,' said Miles, with a brevity of his own that spoke volumes. 'But it's good for Melanie that he still considers himself part of the family—'

He broke off as his wife came down the crushed-stone pathway, accompanied by a plump little girl in a blue swimsuit with a thin towel wrapped around her waist, her wet plait dripping down over her shoulder, her round spectacles glinting in the sun.

'Veronica—how wonderful to see you!' Melanie's clear voice rang out across the garden as she approached in a characteristic rush of enthusiasm, her cool, floral dress fashionably smart on a matronly figure that attested to her love of good food. She ruefully flapped her right arm helplessly in its blue sling and threw her left arm wide, going on tiptoes to offer a welcoming half-hug, laughing at the great disparity in their statures that forced Veronica to bend her knees.

'Oh, but we must do this the French way,' she said, and gave Veronica a brief kiss on both cheeks, and then another peck on the left. 'The third one demonstrates that you're an extra good friend—' her blue eyes twinkled as she backed off, her ash-blonde hair framing a face whose rounded contours were cheerfully unadorned, and remarkably girlish for a woman of nearly fifty '—which you most definitely are, Veronica, to step into the breach like this…poor Karen was terrified I was going to ask her for the ultimate sacrifice! Can you *believe* my horrendously rotten timing? I tripped over a silly *kerb*, of all things, when I was running after something I'd left in the bally car, and hit my elbow on a bollard. I'd just met Miles and Mum and Sophie at the airport. Poor Sophie saw me go shooting past her like a speeding bullet, didn't you, Soph?'

'A speeding bullet smacking into a wall,' the girl said with ghoulish accuracy as her mother paused for a breath. 'Hi, Veronica.' She held out a slightly damp hand, and Veronica politely shook it, hiding her smile as she looked down into the solemn little face.

'Hello, Sophie. It's been ages, hasn't it? I don't think I've seen you more than once or twice since you went off to boarding school and that was—what—nearly two years ago? I hear you got an extension of your school holidays to come to France?'

'Yes, but I still have to do the work, and have it marked when I get back. I don't mind, really—I don't want to fall behind the others.'

'That's not likely—Sophie's way out on top of her class,' said Melanie smugly. 'My late baby is a very early bloomer!'

'Congratulations,' Veronica said to Sophie, who didn't look the least bit smug, just ever so slightly anxious at her mother's boasting. 'One of the burdens of brightness, huh, having to constantly beat off all that praise?'

Sophie's air of gravity lifted at the dry comment, dimples forming in her plump cheeks as she grinned at Veronica with approval, her eyes bright behind their glass shields.

'Obviously the school has worked out well, then,' Veronica commented to Melanie, recalling the anguished soul-searching that Karen had reported going on in the Reed household when the idea was first mooted.

'Yes, but it was Sophie who was determined to go,' said

Miles, giving her soggy braid a squeeze. 'I don't think our feeble brains were providing her enough of an intellectual challenge at home.'

'Oh, *Dad*!' the girl groaned at his teasing.

'Come on, Shrimp, you can't go dripping all over the cottage. Let Mum show Veronica around, and perhaps you can see her again later.'

'Oh, yes—you will come over and have dinner with all of us tonight, won't you, Veronica?' said Melanie confidently.

'Uh, ah, well…' She immediately felt the awkwardness that she had feared would shadow her visit. Did Melanie think that she *had* to invite her over because she was by herself? 'I really wasn't planning on much dinner. I had rather a big lunch…'

'Oh, but—'

'Melanie,' her husband cut her off with laughing affection, 'give the girl some breathing room. Veronica would probably appreciate a little time to settle in, and maybe relax and do her own thing on her first night…'

'Oh, of course, how thoughtless of me—we're going to be pestering enough of you as it is.' Melanie was instantly apologetic as her husband and daughter retreated along the path.

'But you must at least drop over for a pre-dinner drink and a few nibbles, so I can give you all the gen about the area and the village opening hours and best places to eat—say, about six?' she suggested, opening the glass door to the cottage. 'It's a tradition at the Mas when anyone rents the cottage, so Miles can't claim I'm putting undue pressure on you, and it'll give you a chance to say a casual hello to whoever's around.'

Although there was no air-conditioning, it was cooler inside the cottage than out, which Melanie attributed to the traditional, thick-walled construction of the cottage, although it was of relatively modern vintage. To keep the temperature more or less constant she advised Veronica to leave the windows open with the shutters loosely folded across them to provide maximum ventilation and protection from the sun's penetrating heat. 'They've all got insect screens on them, so you can leave the windows open all night, too,' she added.

The well-equipped kitchen and the rustically furnished living area were part of the same large square room, the pale walls and sloping, beamed ceiling high overhead adding to the illusion of space, even though the area was quite compact. Large, dark orange terracotta tiles were cool underfoot and led through to the large bedroom with its matching twin beds and adjoining bathroom, which also housed a washing machine.

'I've left you some milk in the fridge, and there's tea and coffee sachets in the basket on the bench,' Melanie said as she headed back out the door a few minutes later. 'If you do want to go up to the village, it's only a two-minute walk turning right at the end of the vineyard and you've got a butcher, two groceries and three bread shops, so plenty of choice.' She suddenly halted. 'Oh, I just remembered the pool—feel free to use it whenever you like…follow the driveway down to the house and then turn left through the stone archway.' She beamed at Veronica. 'Just wander up around six and you'll find us sitting out in the kitchen courtyard, under the vines. Or shall I send Sophie?'

'To winkle me out?' Veronica raised her eyebrows and Melanie laughed.

'You needn't feel shy,' she said. 'You know most of us already, although not everyone's turned up yet. Ashley's here, of course…she arrived a few days ago with her fiancé—she's been working at a gallery in Melbourne while she continues her art studies. I'm sure she'll be pleased to see you again— and to have another young woman around.'

Veronica smiled noncommittally. She had never particularly warmed to the younger girl on the few occasions they had met, but perhaps she had outgrown her snootiness.

'And Justin?' she asked of Ashley's twin, who had always been the opposite—very amiable and easy to like.

'He's getting the train up from Rome in a few days—he's been working as a chef in a restaurant there. Oops—listen how time flies,' she said as the village bells performed their full carillon followed by the striking of the hour. 'Must go back and see how Mum's getting on with the apple tarts.' Her 'see you later' and 'don't bother to dress up' wafted behind her on the sun-soaked air.

After she had unpacked, Veronica made herself a cup of tea and sprawled on the sunlounger under a leafy tree in the walled garden, leafing through the stack of tourist brochures that had been left in the cottage. She had been intending to cool off with a swim but she fell into a doze and when she woke up it was nearly five o'clock so she decided to walk into the village and stock up on something for breakfast next morning as well as for dinner…not that she was particularly hungry after the trout with almonds she had eaten for lunch at a shady, riverside restaurant beside a giant waterwheel.

The little grocery in the main street had everything that she needed, so she bought sun-ripened melon, warm fuzzy apricots and tiny raspberries to go with her yoghurt in the morning, and a sampling of local fresh cheeses for her dinner along with a bottle of wine, stopping last at the *boulangerie* nearest the cottage to buy a small loaf of crusty bread.

When it was approaching six she had a silky-cool shower and washed her hair, confident it would dry within minutes in the heat, and, hoping that she could take Melanie at her word, slipped into a sleeveless green top and loose white muslin pants and thrust her feet into a pair of good old Kiwi Jandals.

When the clock-tower began to ring she was just stepping onto the driveway and Sophie trotted into view from the direction of the big house, wearing a tee shirt and baggy shorts. 'Mum said I had to wait for the bells to start before I came,' she said, pink-faced from her jog. 'Wait 'til you see what Gran brought back from her friend's place for you.'

'I don't think I *can* wait,' said Veronica with a smile, seeing she was practically bursting from the effort of withholding the news.

'Her friend has a *snail farm*,' Sophie said in tones of awe. 'There are thousands of them from babies to big ones. You can go there and watch them feeding, just like in a zoo.'

'Really?' Veronica's stomach gave a little lurch.

Her face must have given her away because Sophie said kindly: 'They don't really have much taste, you know, but they're a bit chewy. If you pick a little one you can swallow it down real quick.'

'Thanks for the tip, kid.' She grinned as they walked past the stone pavilion that served as a garage and around by the row of young olive trees at the side of the house.

It wasn't until they had stepped into sight of the group of people sitting in various casual attitudes around a large table on a sun-dappled terrace that Veronica suddenly registered what it was that she had seen out of the corner of her eye, parked in between two family saloons.

A streamlined silver convertible with red upholstery!

CHAPTER FOUR

'Ross and Ashley got engaged four months ago,' Melanie was saying as she set out a dish of black and green olives, amongst the tomatoes, roasted peppers and cluster of wine-glasses on the blue and yellow striped tablecloth. 'Ross's in the finance department of a big international bank. He's expecting a posting to New York or London in the next few months, so we'll probably be seeing even less of Ashley than we do now.'

'Oh, really,' murmured Veronica, struggling to maintain the minimum of polite interest when all her attention was focused elsewhere, on the tall, dark-haired man emerging from the dimness of the house, one arm slung around the thin, wiry figure of Zoe Main, the other loosely carrying an opened bottle of red wine.

She was hardly aware of Ross Bentley's winning smile as he shook her hand, or the wheat-blond hair and golden eyes that added the gilt to his chunky good looks. Nor did she notice that the clasp of his hand lingered slightly too long as she failed to flatter him with her full attention, but his sharp-eyed fiancée did.

'Veronica—perhaps it's only an optical illusion, but you seem to have grown taller since we last saw each other,' Ashley drawled from her comfortable seat at the far end of the table, the large diamond ring on her finger sparking in the sunlight as she deliberately moved her wineglass out of a patch of shade thrown by the vines twining the overhead lattice.

'The taller the woman, the more there is to appreciate,' Ross Bentley said in a suave murmur, which would have made Veronica cringe if she had actually been listening.

'I understand that Melanie is insisting we observe local custom, so this is obligatory at the first meeting,' he raised his voice to add with a smooth laugh, putting his hands on her upper arms and making a charming production of bussing her on both cheeks. Since he was several inches shorter than Veronica it made for a slightly awkward manoeuvre as she remained stiffly upright, staring past his head, only vaguely aware of the moist smear of his lips against her pale cheeks.

Visions of mortification danced in her head as she watched the pair moving away from the house. If only she could faint!

But she had a constitution that was as strong as her build, and although it felt as if much of the blood had drained out of her brain she could still pull together a few rational thoughts.

One being that if she toppled over now, she might well take the hovering golden boy down with her, which would give Ashley even more reason to pout.

She could *pretend* to feel faint, and blame it on the heat, but, knowing Melanie, she wouldn't be able to simply totter her way back to the cottage, a handkerchief discreetly pressed to her face, but would be instantly sat down and very publicly fussed over.

Besides, it was too late to avoid the confrontation looming out of the old stone farmhouse, for Lucien was looking right at her—or, more precisely, looking at her and Ross Bentley, his eyes narrowing as they flicked back and forth, his features cast into a dangerously unreadable stillness.

'Luc, I wondered where you'd got to…come over and meet Karen's sister.' Melanie removed the bottle of wine from his hand, giving it to Miles to pour while she one-handedly shepherded her mother and her companion over to where Veronica was standing, shoulders squared as if she were facing a firing squad.

She had a sinking feeling that she knew who he was, far too late for it to do her any good.

Veronica's grey eyes latched onto Zoe's bright, bird-like gaze and she concentrated hard on blocking out all knowledge of her impending humiliation.

'H-hello, Zoe.' She stumbled to get her clumsy tongue around the innocuous words, pushing them out in a rush. 'Karen told me your birthday was coming up, but not that it was such a milestone one—' Another black mark against her sister.

Zoe waved her words away with an acerbic laugh. 'Oh, please, let's forget about that until next week when I *have* to think about it!'

'No one would believe it to look at you, anyway,' managed Veronica, trying not to feel the searing heat of a concentrated brown stare lasering holes in her wafer-thin composure.

It was true. Melanie had said her mother was a lifelong golfer and gardener, and she looked the part—a spritely, nut-brown, vigorous woman who rarely permitted any concessions to her age. Even her short, no-nonsense white hair seemed to vibrate with energy.

'I suppose you're going to tell me I don't look a day over seventy-four, which is what this silver-tongued rascal had the nerve to say!' said Zoe, with a fond frown at the man at her side.

Now there was no more avoiding it. Slowly Veronica turned her unwilling gaze to meet that of her erstwhile lover. He was dressed all in white—crumpled pants and a carelessly buttoned short-sleeved shirt—but his aura was pulsing with ominous darkness.

Stay away from me and mine...

'Veronica, this is my stepson, Lucien Ryder,' Melanie was

saying with an odd mixture of pride and diffidence. 'Luc lived with us for a few years before Sophie was born—until he went to Oxford University on a scholarship when he was sixteen. He stayed on in Europe after he graduated, doing as brilliantly at business as he did at university—but for all that he still considers himself a Kiwi at heart!'

Oh, God, she had chosen to have her wild, anonymous fling with Melanie's stepson!

She had speculated that he might be British or Canadian, but never in a million years had Veronica dreamed that her ex-citingly exotic Frenchman would turn out to be one of her own *countrymen*—a common-or-garden New Zealander! Veronica felt an absurd sense of betrayal. How he must have been laughing at her in Paris!

Lucien made no pretence of politely shaking her hand. He went straight for the jugular, sliding his arms around her back and drawing her against his chest, kissing her cheeks with leisurely deliberation once, twice, three times, aiming the light brush of his mouth just below her ear lobe in each case, where he knew from experience she was ultra-sensitive to a caressing touch.

As a greeting it might have borne an outward resemblance to a sexless salute between new acquaintances, but the message transmitted to her senses was far from innocent. The lazy, rubbing motion of his jaw was like being scent-marked by a big cat and Veronica gave a little, soundless squeak, emerging flushed and breathless as he dropped his arms, but remained threateningly close.

Zoe coughed as Melanie continued rather uncertainly with her introduction, 'Luc, this is Karen's sister, Veronica, who Karen said very kindly leapt into the breach as soon as she heard about my crisis, and insisted on being my substitute right arm while I'm assembling the research for this new book...'

I did? I am? Veronica was too dazed to question this distortion of the facts, while Zoe's second cough sounded more like a smothered laugh.

'*Bonsoir, M'mselle Veronica.*' The slow and lazy intonation combined with the gleam of malice in the dark brown eyes set alarm signals pinging all over her body, his use of French setting her teeth on edge, particularly the heavily accented version of her name. So what if he made it sound sinfully sexy?

'*Kia ora, Lucien,*' she pointedly responded with the traditional Kiwi salutation, trying to pitch her voice to the level of casual amusement without letting it tip over into sarcasm.

Melanie rushed in to fill the pause before it threatened to become awkward. 'We weren't expecting Luc for another couple of days but he arrived a little while before you did, Veronica—and promptly crashed out on his bed! And no wonder he's exhausted—this is his first real break in years. He works too hard in my opinion, and, on top of all that high-pressure living, he now has all this added stress—' She broke off, biting her lip and casting a guilty look at her stepson.

'Don't worry, Melanie, I have a tried-and-true method of coping with pressure,' he interposed smoothly, not taking his eyes off Veronica's pale face, watching the colour mount her face as he said: 'You might call it one of man's most cherished stress-relievers.'

'Don't tell me you've at last taken my advice and started doing yoga—'

'Don't be naïve, Mel, he's a twenty-nine-year-old male in his full-blooded prime—he's talking about sex,' cackled Zoe.

'Oh.' Melanie looked flustered, and then slightly alarmed. 'You didn't—you haven't been getting yourself any *deeper* into complications, have you?' she ventured tentatively.

'Not the kind you're worrying about, no,' he said, to her evident relief. 'I've been out of London for the past few days, remember.'

'Oh, of course—you decided to forget your flights and

come down via Paris instead. So you and Veronica must have been staying there at the same time, Luc—it's a wonder you didn't run across each other. It's because Luc owns an apartment in the building that he heard the short-term rental was coming up for sale and persuaded us to buy it as a good investment,' she told Veronica, who hadn't realised that the Reeds owned the Paris apartment themselves. 'He got it at a marvellous price for us. He's such a cut-throat negotiator...'

'And yet he looks so harmless.' She couldn't help the sarcastic comment. He was still looking at her with that bone-melting intensity, like a predator contemplating a tasty morsel.

'I'm just a big pussy-cat,' he purred at her, as if he could read her mind. 'Actually, Veronica and I did have a brief encounter in the rue de Birague yesterday,' he said, with what she briefly mistook for appalling candour. 'She wanted to know the best place to watch the fireworks...'

'Oh, what a pity you didn't tell us about your change of plans, Luc. I could have suggested you take Veronica under your wing,' said Melanie innocently. 'It was her first time in Paris, you know.'

'I rather gathered that from her schoolgirl attempts to communicate.'

Veronica's lips tightened at the deliberate goad. 'I thought your stepson was French, and at the time he didn't see fit to enlighten me.'

While Melanie looked disconcerted at the revelation, Zoe's eyes narrowed shrewdly. 'So that's why you pokered up when he said hello? Don't take it personally, girl, he was probably just trying to keep an extra-low profile, and that's not so easy in this day and age. You'd be shocked at the ridiculous lengths some people will go to for money, or their fifteen minutes of fame...'

Oh, no, I wouldn't, thought Veronica with a little shudder. She could only hope that Neil had lost his bid to drag her into the spotlight to relive the embarrassing lowlights of their relationship by the time she flew home.

'Come and try this wine that Luc brought with him, Melanie,' Miles broke in, drawing them over to the table where he sat with Ashley and Ross, sipping at a pale rosé. 'It's a local one. I think it might be worth a mention in your book.'

As Ross contributed his opinion as a self-proclaimed expert Luc linked arms with Zoe to escort her to her chair and Veronica jumped as his other hand hooked under her elbow, his sun-warmed arm sliding against hers as he anchored her to his side.

'Relax,' he murmured, inclining his head until a loose strand of jet-black hair drifted to cling against the mahogany tresses falling in smooth layers around her face. 'Don't be so jumpy, or you'll make them suspicious.'

She was the one who was suddenly suspicious. 'I thought you wanted me to rue the day,' she muttered out of the corner of her mouth.

'Ah, but that's when I thought you were some ratbag freelance journalist out to get me.'

'I'd already *got* you,' she couldn't help retorting.

'But you weren't scheming to sell me down the river over it…you really *hadn't* looked at that newspaper. You had no idea who I was until just now.' Even in an undertone his voice was rich with a gloating satisfaction. He took such pleasure in her ignorance that she was perversely annoyed.

'Didn't I?' she murmured unwisely, savouring the way his head snapped sideways as she pulled her arm free and quickly slipped onto the empty chair between Sophie and Melanie. Serve him right for suspecting her in the first place.

To her frustration he waited until she was seated before dragging an empty chair around and squeezing it in between her and Sophie, hitching it forward with little bunny-hops of his legs that had the little girl in giggles as she was shunted into making room for him. Perforce, Veronica had to ease aside also, but not far enough to avoid the constant, casual brush of his shoulder and the not-so-casual shift of his hard calf against hers beneath the hanging tablecloth.

Although Veronica guessed she must not have seen him very often in her young life, Sophie obviously thought the world of Luc, for after a shy start she was soon peppering him with questions, to which he patiently responded.

'Luc has been sending her regular emails at school,' Melanie confided to Veronica, 'ever since she wrote to him a few years ago. I didn't know if he'd find the time to reply, let alone bother to keep it up, but he's been absolutely marvellous, even helping her with some of her school assignments... which is more than her sister ever did for her,' she added, with a pointed look across the table.

'Luc's the genius, it's easy for him,' said Ashley carelessly. 'I was never any good at ordinary schoolwork. I'm the artistic type—I work on the visual plane.'

'You could still find time to write occasionally, and not only to Sophie...'

'What with having to work in the gallery and studying and constantly working towards my next exhibition—not to mention all Ross's social obligations—I don't *have* any spare time,' was the plaintive reply.

'What kind of painting do you do?' asked Veronica politely.

Ashley gave her a patronising look. 'I'm not a *painter*. I don't restrict myself to revisiting dead conventions; I'm an environmental constructionist—I conceptualise space and remodel it with mixed-media and sculptural forms.'

'Ashley is an installation artist,' translated Luc, taking pity on Veronica's look of confusion. 'You know the kind of thing— covering objects in bubble-wrap, running hours of looped video in a room with the furniture glued to the ceiling...'

'Oh, sorry, Ashley, I really don't know much about modern

art,' Veronica said humbly, thinking it sounded quite ghastly. 'I did enjoy the Picasso Museum in Paris, though.'

Her attempt to find common ground went down like a lead balloon. 'Oh, *Picasso*—he's accessible to pretty well everyone these days.' Ashley shrugged.

'Ashley prides herself on her inaccessibility,' said Luc, his voice so exquisitely deadpan that Veronica glanced sideways at him, and almost made the mistake of laughing.

Ashley's pretty face tensed, her blue eyes narrowing in fleeting doubt under the funky fringe of her bleached blonde hair before she decided to take the comment at its face value. 'The struggle to be understood is part of the challenge of being on the cutting edge of art,' she declared loftily.

'Installation art is a hot-button for sponsorship in the Melbourne cultural scene at the moment,' contributed Ross, pouring himself another glass of wine and reaching for the olives. 'If you can get yourself noticed you can virtually write your own cheques. If I get posted to London, Ryder, perhaps you might be able to use some of your financial connections to help get sponsorship for an exhibition of Ash's work,' he said to Lucien, with an ingratiating smile that suggested he was well aware of the potential value of such contacts to himself.

'Perhaps.' Lucien's voice was pleasant but noncommittal and Veronica, acutely attuned to every nuance of his tone, sensed his instinctive dislike of the other man.

Ashley flushed.

'Luc's got billions, he could afford to sponsor me himself, if he wasn't such a philistine,' she said, with a careless toss of her head.

'No, he hasn't, he's only a millionaire,' piped up Sophie. 'I looked it up on the web. A billion is a thousand million and Luc only has—'

'Sophie!' her mother said sharply. 'It's rude to talk how much money people have right in front of them.'

'That's right, you should be like everyone else and do it sneakily, behind my back,' grinned Lucien, giving Sophie a wink and making Melanie pinken.

'Ashley said it first,' the little girl was emboldened to say, 'and she made a mistake, so I *had* to say something. Anyway, that's what Luc *does*…he talks to people all the time about how much money they have and how much of his money they need to make their things work. That's not rude, that's just business.'

'She means I'm a venture capitalist,' said Lucien, catching the flicker of Veronica's dark lashes. 'I invest in other people's ideas.'

He made it sound as simple as putting money in the bank, but Veronica knew that if he was making millions he was either incredibly astute or fantastically lucky…or a combination of both.

'That's a very high-risk field, isn't it?' she felt compelled to ask, wondering if a controversial investment gone wrong was the reason he was ducking the press.

He shrugged. 'No risk, no gain—surely you subscribe to that philosophy yourself…' It was a statement, not a question, the sensuality sheathed in his slow smile hinting of things that had nothing to do with finance.

Veronica chose to ignore the sly suggestions. 'What kind of ideas do you invest in?'

'Whatever happens to interest me at the time. I'm a maverick.' His shoulder brushed her arm as he stretched across the table to snag the bottle that Ross had left at his elbow and offer to top up her almost-empty glass.

'Oh, I don't know that I should—' she said weakly, denying the temptation offered by the deliciously chilled nectar. She hadn't been drunk last night, but she had certainly been uninhibited. She didn't dare risk the reappearance of the wild, wanton woman she thought that she had left in Paris.

'Go on, say yes, you know you want it,' Lucien said silkily, tilting the bottle and emptying it into her glass. 'Don't deny yourself pleasure just because you think it might be bad for you. Sometimes bad is very, very good.'

His words shivered over her, something warm and heavy coiling and uncoiling in her stomach. She was beginning to realise that she had made a silly mistake in not instantly acknowledging she'd spent the evening in his company, and laughing it off to the Reeds as just one of those crazy things. That would have been the mature, sophisticated thing to do. Instead, by hiding it, she had made it into something more important than it was, an intimate secret between the two of them, compounding her embarrassment if it ever came out—and handing Luc a licence to torment her for his own amusement.

'Yes, you'd better have something to wash down the *you-know-what*,' Sophie reminded her. 'Didn't you say you had something for Veronica, Gran?' she urged.

'Ah, yes, the Mas de Bonnard rite of passage,' intoned Miles, lifting a little covered pottery dish painted in the bright colours of Provence and passing it along the table to his mother-in-law.

'Fred and I used to come here on holiday every winter for years,' said Zoe reminiscently as she cradled the dish. 'We loved it so much we were even talking about buying Mas de Bonnard and retiring here to run a B&B—we ran a motel, you see, and Fred was a cook. He died just before his sixty-fifth birthday, but I knew he wouldn't want me to stop coming, so I've been making it a kind of pilgrimage ever since. We have lots of friends here amongst the locals over the years, which is why we know where to go for the best of everything and dear Fred did love his marinated snails…'

There was evidently no escaping her initiation, and Veronica was the cynosure of all eyes as she took up a toothpick and dutifully paid her tribute to Fred, chewing her way through the small, chilled delicacy, relieved to discover that all she could taste was the spicy marinade, the boiled snail having a texture similar to squid. Out of sheer bravado, because she sensed Lucien thought she wouldn't, she even ate a second, but hastily waved away his sly offer to fetch her a plate.

'Now you're one of us,' said Sophie, with satisfaction. 'I bet Karen wouldn't have done it. She'd have squealed and claimed it was too yucky.' She obviously remembered how fastidious her former nanny had been about food.

'Or complained about the number of calories,' smiled Veronica.

That brought the conversation around to Karen's foray into modelling and from Melanie's comments it was obvious that, far from giving her sister a choice, Karen had freely offered Veronica's services before she had ever arrived in England. It was Melanie who had been dubious about encroaching on Veronica's holiday and Karen who had earnestly assured her that it was no problem, for Veronica considered it in the nature of a working vacation anyway, and the free accommodation ample compensation for her time.

Veronica saw little point in revealing how Karen had twisted the facts to suit herself. Even if she wanted to turn tail and run at the daunting prospect of seeing Lucien each day, she knew she was well and truly trapped by her own sense of responsibility.

It was the same strong sense of duty that had kept her hostage on her parents' farm when she had envisaged a very different future for herself.

'How convenient for Karen,' Lucien was commenting. 'You know, you'll probably have to look for a new assistant soon anyway, if she's really been bitten by the modelling bug and not just doing it for a bit of fun.'

'I know, but I don't even want to have to *think* about it just yet,' said Melanie. 'Karen's always fitted in so well...but I knew there'd come a time when she'd get restless and want to move on, and the job is changing, too. There's less personal and more office work involved now, which I know isn't really her thing…'

But a certain inflection in Lucien's voice along with the aptness of his observation had brought Veronica's head around. 'Do you *know* Karen?'

His eyelids drooped, thick black lashes veiling his gaze. 'We've met a few times when she's been in London with Melanie.' And before another question could form in her mind, let alone her tongue, he added, 'If you're here on a working holiday, what is it exactly that you do, Veronica?'

'I thought you were some kind of accountant for your parents,' said Ashley languidly, making it sound like a sinecure. 'Except—didn't Karen say you weren't actually qualified?'

'I'm not a chartered accountant, if that's what you mean,' said Veronica evenly. 'I left school to help Mum and Dad sell fresh produce from their organic farm, and took accounting courses by correspondence so I could handle their bookkeeping. Gradually I started doing the books for other friends and neighbours with rural small businesses as well.' Because her parents hadn't been able to afford to pay her, she had had to invent ways to earn herself some money and contribute to the household expenses, inadvertently providing herself with the means and incentive to finally assert her independence.

She had loved school and longed to go on to university, but at the time her parents had been struggling, so she had quietly put her dreams of an independent career on hold and stayed home on the farm. As their first-born it was taken for granted that she would be a pillar of strength. Her sister and brother were years younger and had still had to finish their schooling. Her hard-working parents hadn't quite known how they had managed to produce such an ethereal beauty as Karen between sensible, brainy Veronica and brawny, down-to-earth

John—who was a farmer from the day he could first stick his chubby toddler's foot in a gumboot. So when the organic food trade had begun to take off and their money problems had eased a little, it was effervescent Karen, scraping through with minimum marks, who had been allowed to go straight from school to university in Auckland, even though she had no real ambition to study, and had dropped out the instant the Reeds had offered her a full-time job looking after Sophie.

'Now that organically grown food is in such big demand globally, your parents must be glad that they were in the vanguard of the revolution,' said Melanie knowledgeably, picking up a paper fan to direct a cooling breeze through her gauze sling. 'Bell Farm has got itself a solid reputation for quality goods.'

'Karen showed me the website for the farm that you designed. It's very impressive,' said Miles, pulling the cork out of another bottle of wine. 'She said you took all the photographs for it yourself.'

'It's a hobby of mine.' She shrugged, flushing with pleasure at his praise. 'Bell Farm gets a lot of online orders now, especially for our Christmas gift packs. In fact, that's what gave me the idea for my new business. Now that my parents have hired a new business manager and my brother has left school to work full-time on the farm, I'm moving up to Auckland to concentrate on a mail-order gift-buying service that I've been building up online over the past couple of years.' Her enthusiasm made her temporarily forget her self-consciousness, her freckled face losing its preoccupied reserve and coming alive with eagerness as Miles urged her on with an interested question while Ashley giggled something in Ross's ear.

'It's for corporate and PR purposes as well as people looking for the individual touch, something small but exclusive, handcrafted and distinctive—the kind of curio you don't usually find in shops outside the local area of production. It started off New Zealand-themed, but now I have a few friends who live abroad sourcing items for me, and I've had enough overseas orders to enable me to look at buying from other markets and launching an international online service.'

'Well, you've certainly done the right thing coming here. You'll find plenty of ideas at the local markets around the Vaucluse,' Melanie said, selecting a plump green olive glistening with herb-flecked dressing to pop in her mouth. 'Of course a great deal of what's on offer is far too touristy for your purposes, but there's some really good, genuine craftwork to be had if you strike the right time and place, or go off the beaten track a bit. I'm sure Mum can help you there and, actually, it'll really fit in with much of what I was going to ask you to do, because my new book is going to be a tour of some of the food markets of France and I had planned to dash thither and yon in the car to pick up information and samples from markets and specialty food producers so that I can decide where I want to focus my research.'

It didn't sound too onerous, and Veronica's fears of spending the greater part of the beginning of her holiday in Provence cooped up inside were gratefully dispelled. And besides, Karen would soon be arriving to take back her rightful duties.

'So you're going global,' teased Miles. 'Are you aiming to be New Zealand's next dot.com millionaire?'

'I don't think that's really likely,' smiled Veronica. 'But I've already had some important orders from Kiwi multinational companies.'

'Guts and money, I suppose you must need equal amounts of both to do what you're doing,' Zoe guessed shrewdly.

'Well, it is a bit scary, but in a good way,' Veronica admitted. 'I've been planning it for years so I'm fairly confident I'm not over-extending myself. If things work out I'll probably take on a partner at some point, to free myself up to travel on more buying trips.'

'If you want expert advice you should talk to Luc,' said Melanie. 'He's in a perfect position to know. He made his first fortune in currency speculation and doubled it backing Internet start-ups.'

Veronica immediately felt her skin prickle with renewed tension. For a few minutes she had forgotten the major complication at her side. He had been talking to Sophie, but his swift answer showed that he was perfectly able to multitask.

'You forget that I also lost it all the same way,' said Luc drily.

'Yes, but you were only twenty. You soon made it all back again, and more,' said Melanie proudly. 'Honestly, Veronica, he's invested in new Internet companies all over the world, so he knows what he's talking about. And he's right here, so why not take shameless advantage of his prime area of expertise?'

Veronica thought she already had! Half turned away from him, she heard a smothered laugh that feathered hot breath over her bare shoulder, and was mortified to know that he was thinking the same thing.

'No, really,' she choked. 'Enough people have had their holidays disrupted. I don't want to disturb him on his break—'

'I'm already disrupted and disturbed,' he growled.

'Oh, go on, Luc, it might help stop you brooding about that—about what's happened,' Melanie said, adding in an unfortunate choice of words, 'and give you a chance to sink your teeth back into something that excites you...'

'Mmm, that's very true...' he mused wickedly, and Veronica didn't dare look at him for fear her head would explode with the heat of her blushes, her breasts tingling at the memory of the luscious bites he had used to arouse and appease their mutual hunger. She suddenly felt his hand on her upper arm, his knuckles skimming the tender side of her breast as his fingers curled into her warm skin, tugging her inexorably around to meet his dark, taunting gaze. 'What do you think, Veronica? Do you think you might benefit from a personal demonstration of my…exciting expertise?'

'You see, Veronica?' Melanie said happily. 'Isn't it lucky that you and Luc are down here at the same time? He's usually a very difficult man to pin down. It couldn't have been better if you *planned* for it to happen this way.'

At her words, Luc's fingers tightened on Veronica's soft flesh, his face hardening, throwing his bold nose into sharp relief as his eyebrows lowered over eyes that swarmed with sudden suspicion.

She could read him like a book, she realised in furious exasperation. Now he was actually wondering if it had all been some giant conspiracy on her part.

'Oh, dear—now I'm found out I suppose I should confess that it's not your expertise I'm after, just your money,' she oozed, pouring fuel onto the smouldering fire.

His eyes narrowed and she smiled with lots of teeth.

'I was going to ask for a few million, but now that I know you're not the fabulous billionaire I thought you were, I suppose I'll have to settle for a measly few hundred thousand. If you could make the cheque out to cash,' she suggested sweetly, 'I'll bank it straight into my numbered Swiss account.'

'Very amusing,' he grunted as the rest of the table responded to the joke.

She rounded her widely spaced grey eyes and made a show of nibbling on her lower lip. 'But…don't you believe me?'

His fingers trailed down to rest in the sensitive crease of her inner elbow, lightly teasing at the nerve endings. 'I *believe* you're playing a dangerous game…and wonder if you've considered all the consequences…'

Of course she hadn't, she had got carried away by the sheer exhilaration of paying him back for his unworthy suspicions. His suggestive threat made her realise that she had just done the equivalent of putting her head in the lion's mouth and Veronica quickly withdrew it, throwing out a question to Zoe about the St Romain, which turned the conversation general and allowed her to sink back into polite silence.

A little while later she excused herself with the plea of being tired, and agreed to join Melanie for coffee late in the morning to discuss her plans for the next few days.

As she was leaving Zoe pressed on her a jar of fresh apricot jam, which she had made to an old Provence recipe with fruit harvested from the trees in the garden, to have with her breakfast.

'Oh, are you allowed to pick the fruit?' said Veronica, thinking of the laden branches of the greengage tree beside the cottage.

Zoe's sun-creased face split in a rapturous smile. 'The owners always let me do a bit in the gardens while I was here and take what little I wanted to use for myself, but now I don't have to even think about it. Luc bought Mas de Bonnard a few months ago and is insisting on signing it over to me as a birthday present, extravagant lad that he is—not that I've agreed to accept it, yet…'

'Liar.' The extravagant boy grinned, getting lazily to his feet. 'You've already got Miles doing renovations and Melanie planning to set a book here. You're going to love being able to come and go as you please—you can spend the whole of the New Zealand winter here, if you like—and I'll bet there'll never be any shortage of family and friends to keep you company.'

Veronica had thought he was only standing up to be polite, or to stretch his long limbs, but instead he started to turn when she did.

'I'll walk down with you. I need to get something from my car,' he said casually as she opened her mouth to reject the need for an escort.

'Could you go round by way of the pool?' said Melanie.

'I meant to show Veronica where it was. No, *not* you, Sophie, I want you to help Ashley get the table set and the vegetables ready for dinner, and no face-pulling either of you, you know what the deal is—while I'm in this sling I can't lift things out of the oven, or chop safely.'

Veronica barely glanced at the inviting blue waters of the big, rectangular swimming pool, walking briskly around the white-paved edge and along the winding path through the shrubbery, past a huge vegetable garden next to a big, stone cistern of water and back onto a recognisable part of the drive-way, her nervousness heightened by Luc's brief directions framed in deafening silence.

She was surprised and relieved when he turned out to have been telling the truth and peeled off towards his parked car, leaving Veronica to quicken her pace and hurry off to the cottage, entering it with a thumping heart, and the feeling that she had just dodged a bullet.

She went into the deep recess of the bathroom and splashed water on her flushed face, leaving the dewy sheen of droplets to evaporate on her skin. Outside the sun was still shining as it dropped lower in the cloudless sky, radiating heat to the baked earth, but the drawn shutters made the interior of the cottage soothingly dim, so that when she first came out of the bedroom raking her hands through her thick hair to lift it away from her hot scalp, she didn't immediately see the man braced against the frame of the sliding door she had left open to the faint breeze.

She gasped as she saw the shimmer of his white clothes and his brown arms flex as he shifted stance, leaning in across the threshold.

'Why so shocked? Surely you were expecting me. Did you really think I was going to let you off that easily?'

CHAPTER FIVE

'YOU can't come in!' Veronica blurted as he straightened up to step inside.

Lucien rested the hilt of his shoulder against the door, thrusting one hand into his trouser pocket, studying the woman who was the first in a very long time to confuse and confound him. Maybe it was the freckles, he brooded. They gave her an erroneous air of innocent playfulness, which his jaded senses had found irresistibly appealing. In fact, she had slipped under his well-protected guard with unsettling ease considering that he had already been on high alert after his nasty brush with notoriety in London. But although that situation had blown up in his face and given him a literal as well as a figurative bloody nose, it hadn't shocked him to his cynical core—unlike his passionate run-in with the not-so-innocent seductress poised front of him, her body a symphony of curves beneath her summery-thin clothes.

He had the advantage of knowing exactly what she looked like without them…a life model for one of the great painters of sensuous female nudes.

Not Rubens, but Renoir, he decided, his imagination winging back to his Paris apartment to view his impressionistic memory of her reclining against the disordered pillows, her smooth skin rosy with a delicious warmth, her opulent breasts firm with excitement, their soft pink tips peaking with pleasure as he played with them, her lush hips and rounded limbs gilded by the light of the lamp, welcoming the weight of his big body as he wrestled her into eager submission and thrust into her tight, sultry heat.

He felt the hot stirring in his groin with a savage amusement, embracing the surge of predatory lust that powered his male desire to hunt, capture and dominate and refocused his wandering thoughts on his most immediate goal.

'Why can't I?' he challenged, content for the moment to indulge her naïve belief that she was in control, for the sheer anticipated pleasure of proving otherwise. 'You left your door wide-open, so you must have been expecting me to follow you…'

Veronica's fingers contracted against her scalp in instinctive rejection of the Freudian possibility that she had *wanted* him to invade her private space.

'I left it open for the breeze—'

'And whatever the breeze blows in,' he pointed out, his lazy smile belied by his watchful intent. 'It's not as if I'm a stranger. As you can see, I'm just the boy from next door.'

His darkening eyes swept over her and Veronica was suddenly made aware of her upraised arms and unconsciously provocative pose. She wrenched her hands down from her head, wincing as they took with them several tangled strands of hair.

'Or is that the problem?' he guessed wryly, boosting himself off the door and sauntering inside in brazen defiance of her expressed command. 'You're embarrassed to admit that you had a wild sex romp with the boy next door.'

'You sound like a cheap tabloid newspaper headline,' she snapped, instinctively jabbing at the place she thought he would be most vulnerable.

'I've just had a crash course,' he said with a grim smile.

'And believe me, the tabloids are anything but cheap when they're shelling out for sleaze.'

'Well, thankfully that's outside my experience.'

'And what's *inside* your experience? Picking up anonymous foreigners in bars for—well, what would *you* prefer to call it…a "torrid night of passion"?'

Veronica clenched her hands at her sides. Did he really think she was that shamefully indiscriminate? 'I—you—'

'Yes, you and I,' he cut through her faltering attempt to fend off his barrage, 'burning up the sheets together. And now you seem to want to act as if we never met. What frightens you more, Veronica—the fact that I'm a real person and not some obedient sexual fantasy-figure tucked away in your memories, or the fact that I've turned out to be someone you can't just walk away from?'

She hunched her shoulders. It was his bruised male ego talking, she told herself, that was all. 'I—it should never have happened,' she said, moving over to pick up the apricot jam she had left by the sink and put it in the small under-bench refrigerator.

'But it did happen, and I'm a naturally curious person, I want to know why,' he pressed ruthlessly on her squirming conscience. 'Why don't you want to talk about it? Am I breaking some kind of taboo? Do you have some kinky fetish about bedding men who can only use a foreign tongue, so to speak?'

Her cheeks pinkened at his crude innuendo and she grabbed up a cloth and began to wipe down the spotless bench. 'No! Of course not—I'm not in the habit of *bedding* anyone—'

'You mean this was the first time for you?' he asked cynically, planting his hip against the edge of the bench, effectively preventing her from continuing her pointless busy-work.

'Yes—I mean, no,' she added hastily, in case he thought she was trying to claim to have been a virgin. She threw down the cloth and drilled him with a defiant glare. 'I don't see why I should have to answer any more of your insulting questions. My love life is none of your business—'

'*Love* life?' His eyebrows shot up and she cursed herself for that unthinking choice of words. 'Interesting that you find it insulting that I seek to understand how I fit into your...*love life*. As for questions—well, isn't there one *you've* been wanting to ask *me*?'

Her heart began to thud unevenly in her breast, her breathing growing choppy. Questions could sometimes be as revealing as answers.

'About this, for example.' He withdrew his hand from his trouser pocket and she uttered a croaky little sound as he opened it to show her the jade pendant lying in his open palm. 'I'd strung it from the rear-vision mirror of the car, to remind me to steer clear of perfidious jades,' he said with gentle malice. 'I found it in my bed in Paris—it has a damaged catch, otherwise I might have been left to wonder if you'd been a figment of my over-heated imagination. Pretty, isn't it? Yet cruel in what it actually represents—a vicious hook on which to snag an unsuspecting fish and drag the poor, helpless victim to a painful fate.'

She took her eyes off the pendant only long enough to flick him a scathing look—surely he wasn't implying that he was in any way a helpless victim? Or unsuspecting, come to that!

He watched her as he hefted it thoughtfully in his hand. 'Quite valuable, too, I imagine...' he mused with an infuriating smile.

Her hand darted out, but her fingertips barely grazed the delicate chain before his hand snapped shut over his prize, presenting her with an impenetrable fist.

'Or does its sentimental value outweigh the price of the jade? Perhaps it was a romantic gift from a lover—someone you left back in New Zealand?'

She was unwillingly reminded of the modest diamond chip that Neil had demanded back after their failed engagement—

the ring being the only piece of jewellery he had given her during their two-year relationship.

Lucien obviously wasn't going to give the pendant back until she told him. 'My parents gave it to me as a twenty-first birthday present,' she admitted stiffly. 'I don't often take it off, so it's not surprising that I didn't notice that the catch was worn.'

But instead of handing it over he slipped it back into his pocket under her outraged eyes. 'It would be a pity to risk losing it in someone else's bed. They might not be as scrupulous as I am about returning it,' he said glibly.

'You *haven't* returned it,' she was stung to reply.

'There's no point at the moment, since it's unwearable. I thought I'd find a jeweller somewhere and get it fixed for you.'

She didn't believe his innocent look. He was tantamount to holding her pendant hostage to her good behaviour. 'That's not necessary—'

'I know, but I want to do it. Consider it in the nature of an apology.'

'For what?' she said warily, mistrusting his silky sincerity.

'For what I said to you out there on the road, when I thought you were a stalking journalist. I may have gone over the top with some of my remarks—' He paused, watching as the most memorable of them popped back into her head.

'The best lay I've had in a long, long time…'

Then as she visibly fought down her blush of chagrin he added simply: 'About you staying away from me.'

That was all, and her blush exploded out of control as she realised what he was, oh, so clearly *not* apologising for…

'I should have given you the slap you deserved,' she choked.

'Feel free to do it now,' he invited, spreading his arms and taking another step closer, turning his head to present her with an olive-skinned cheek, his drawn-back hair a sleek backdrop to his neatly moulded ear.

'It would serve you right if I did,' she said fiercely, her hand twitching with the temptation to rediscover the feel of that fine-grained skin.

'Try it—perhaps we both might like it,' he urged wickedly, slanting his eyes to meet hers. 'After all, we did have an unexpectedly exciting time together in Paris. It's just a pity you had to rush off the way you did, before we had a chance to fully explore all the pleasurable possibilities…'

Veronica's grey eyes widened in part shock, part curiosity. He had more than fulfilled her fantasies. What, precisely, *hadn't* they explored…?

He shifted to look her full in the face again. 'Not that you gave me any hints that you were interested in anything violent or kinky.' His voice had lowered to that velvety purr she found so disruptive to her thought processes that she didn't notice he had moved even closer. 'You were exquisitely responsive to my lightest touch. So what was it that made you select me to be your partner for the night? What do you look for in a man, in a lover, when you go on the prowl?'

'I wasn't on the *prowl*,' she protested. 'I—I was excited about being in Paris…I just got carried away and so thought I'd—I'd—'

'Find out what a Frenchman was like as a lover?'

Not just any Frenchman. You! she wanted to blurt in her own defence, but the knowledge that it was the truth was too dangerous to admit. His ego was already puffed up; there was no need for him to know how elemental her attraction to him had been from the first moment she had seen him sitting in the café. How she had woven richly embroidered dreams and fantasies around him before she had worked up the courage to make her reckless approach.

'I wasn't looking for a lover,' she denied. 'Just some company for my last night in Paris, and I thought you looked…interesting.'

'But obviously not interesting enough to stick around for

conversation after you'd had your wicked way with me,' he goaded. 'You don't seem to require a very in-depth relationship in your sexual partners.'

'You can talk! I didn't notice you turning down the chance of a one-night stand!' she said hotly.

His eyes gleamed with satisfaction at her response to his inflammatory statement.

'Is that what it was? I thought it was a mutual *coup de foudre*. I assumed that after our exhausting revels, we'd wake up together in the morning…'

'And what? And share a few laughs about how you fooled me into believing you couldn't understand me?' she threw at him.

'Oh, I think that in the heat of the night we understood each other perfectly well,' he drawled with rock-hard confidence. 'You might recall I did let slip quite a few extremely fluent English phrases in your ear while I was inside you, and you told me quite explicitly what you liked about my body and what you wanted me to do with it. And when you begged me to make love to you, I certainly didn't ask for a translation…'

'Did I? I don't remember—' She flushed and turned her back, her arm brushing his body. How and when had she let him get so close?

She realised her strategic error when his arm snaked around her waist, stopping her from walking away.

'Don't you?' His muscled arm slowly contracted, drawing her back against his chest, fitting her bottom into the warm saddle of his hips. 'Are you sure?' he murmured, his hard chin sinking into the hollow between her neck and shoulder, anchoring their upper bodies together.

She shivered at the feel of his lips moving against the side of her bare throat as he continued to speak in that dark, sultry tone: 'I think you'll find that you remember a lot more than you're willing to admit.' His arm was replaced with his big hands spanning the sides of her waist, his fingers slanting down across her hip-bones as he pressed her more snugly against his potent hardness.

'There's no need to feel shy, Veronica,' he whispered with shattering insight. 'See how wonderfully well our bodies are shaped to fit each other. You don't have to be ashamed of what we did together. It was entirely natural…a man and a woman freely expressing their mutual desire. *Je ne regrette rien…*'

She stiffened, wanting to punish him for the accuracy of his perception and at the same time let him know that she wasn't going to make the same mistake twice. No matter how glorious it had felt at the time, the aftermath of her flirtation with fantasy had taught her that she wasn't cut out to be a spontaneous wild-child.

'I'm not *shy*. I know it was just a one-time thing, that it didn't *mean* anything,' she said, trying to sound crushingly sophisticated.

His cheek nuzzled against the side of her throat. 'Are you sure about that?' His hands slipped under the edge of her top, his palms skimming up over her bare skin to cup her breasts in their silky-fine casing of stretchy fabric. 'Don't you remember how good it felt when there was nothing between your skin and mine…when we were naked with each other and I touched you like this…?' His fingers feathered across the centre of her breasts, circling the betraying tightness of her nipples, drawing them out to prominent points against the seamless tee-shirt bra, and capturing them between thumb and forefinger. He turned his open mouth into her neck and scraped her lightly with his teeth and sucking at the thrilling sting. 'Don't you remember saying how you wanted this feeling to go on for ever,' he said huskily, applying delicate pressure and rolling her throbbing nipples between his fingers, 'how you moaned when I took these in my mouth and tasted you for the first time, how you melted with pleasure when I showed you just how exquisitely sensitive you are here, how violently responsive to the lightest stroke of my tongue…?'

Veronica shuddered, arching helplessly back against him as his hands contracted, compressing the pleasure into a dangerous thrill of forbidden delight.

His mouth moved up behind her ear, his breath as hot as his words as he confided how much her eager delight had pleased him. 'It gave me such an incredible rush when I made you come just by devoting myself to your gorgeous breasts, licking and sucking on these sexy, pointed nipples until you went wild in my arms…'

He ignored her choked cry; one of his hands abandoned its lavish attentions and moved down to smooth over her hip and push between their bodies, tracing the generous curve of her bottom to its bisecting crease. 'And here, where you're so lush and round and womanly…' his velvety whisper paused as he sank his teeth lightly into her fleshy ear lobe, his hand adjusting her so that she could feel the thick shaft of muscle lying against her resilient flesh '…remember how I kissed my way down your spine to this highly sensitive spot, the one just here…and then…' Using darkly intense language, he described what he had done with an explicit eroticism that made her squeeze her thighs together in an effort to control the hot pulse of arousal that threatened to melt her into a submissive puddle at his feet.

The involuntary clench of her buttocks gripped him in an intimate clasp, and she felt his groan vibrating from his chest.

'Oh, yes, you liked that, didn't you?' he said thickly, his fingers plunging under the smooth edge of her bra to find her distended nipple while his hips pushed his engorged manhood against the cleft of her bottom, creating an exciting friction in both places that edged her even nearer to a total meltdown. 'You liked everything that we did to each other,' he purred, nibbling at the nape of her neck. 'The trouble was, it was all over so fast we hardly had time to savour it…' He strung a series of light, teasing kisses to the tip of her shoulder, at odds with the simmering tension in his body. 'But here there's no need for us to rush our love-making. We can explore the sensuous side of passion…see if we enjoy slow and lazy as much as fast and furious. Just imagine how much more exciting it could be if we take the time to learn each other's most erotic, most intimate secrets…'

The mention of secrets made Veronica flinch. Where before the romantic fantasy of a mysterious lover had been thrilling, now she knew that where there was no knowledge there was no trust. The real Lucien Ryder was still an enigma to her; a wealthy, worldly sophisticate, prone to high-risk behaviour and embroiled in some nameless trouble. He might not be the psychotic killer of her foolish fears, but he could still turn out to be extremely dangerous to her emotional health.

Now that he had satisfied himself that Veronica wasn't a threat to his own security, Lucien had evidently decided to take advantage of the fact that she was convenient and available, and spin out their one night of 'no regrets' into a 'no strings' holiday affair.

Of course it wouldn't occur to him that she might not be interested in acquiring the questionable status of his temporary lover, she thought, desperately trying to whip up a defensive anger. He talked very persuasively of passion and exploration, but there was no mention of any desire for emotional intimacy in his suggested affair. While he might be able to retain the necessary detachment, Veronica was less sanguine about her chances of walking away with her heart intact. A few hours in his company had already caused her as much turmoil as pleasure, filling her with conflicting doubts and yearnings. She was afraid that with continued exposure she could very easily fall under the spell of his forceful, charismatic personality and end up with a guaranteed heartbreak when he vanished back to his rarefied world.

If she didn't murder him first!

She angled her head away from the ravishing series of kisses he was planting on her bare throat and somehow found the strength to wrench herself out of his seductive embrace.

'I think I asked you to leave—' she rasped, backing hastily away, her shaking hands pulling her clothing straight as she tried to claw back her composure.

To her fury he looked undaunted by the sharp rejection, if anything a hint of amusement entering his dark, brooding gaze. 'Are you saying you're not interested?'

She pushed back her hair, feeling the strands pull where they had clung to the throat he had dampened with his kisses. 'No—' She saw the carnal flame leap in his eyes and quickly corrected herself, 'I mean, yes, I *am* saying that…'

His gaze fell to her swollen breasts, heaving with each shallow, gasping breath, the tightly furled nipples prominent against the thin cotton. His eyelids lowered, covering the glitter of savage satisfaction.

'I think your body begs to differ,' he murmured.

She wanted to wrap her arms over her chest and shield herself from his knowing eyes, but knew it would be seen as an indication of weakness. 'My brain is what runs my life, my body doesn't get a vote,' she said proudly.

His mouth curved sardonically as he took a step forward. 'Oh, no?'

She threw up a desperate, staying hand. 'I don't want you touching me!'

He obediently halted, and looked ruefully down at himself, hooking a casual thumb in the empty belt-loop of his crumpled trousers. 'Well, I guess you can see what *I* want…'

In spite of the fact she knew it was an intentional goad, she couldn't help following his gaze to the bold erection outlined by the white fabric pulled taut over his groin. Just looking at it made her feel hot and dizzy and her lips parted as she sucked in a gulp of sluggish air. To her fevered shock his hand dropped from his belt-loop to adjust the stiffened bulge, easing it to one side of his zip, allowing her to see the outline visibly growing thicker under her fascinated stare.

Cheeks flaming cherry-red, her eyes ripped guiltily back to his face, to find his eyes lying tauntingly in wait.

'Sorry, but I was afraid I was in danger of permanent damage from the teeth of that zip,' he said with extravagant insincerity. 'Of course, if it was *your* teeth around me I'd consider it well worth the risk. It's something we never got around to, but I'm anticipating that might change. You were rather looking at me as if you'd like to eat me up…'

Shock nailed her to the spot. 'I was *not*! I wouldn't—I've never—' Her mouth snapped shut as his sultry expression changed to one of electrified curiosity.

'Never?'

She gave him an excoriating look and stalked to stand beside the door.

When she turned to indicate she was waiting for him to leave he was looking after her with a certain amount of awe, and a sizzling speculation that raised the fine hairs on her arms. He stood for a moment, then reluctantly began to move towards the door. As he came level with her rigid figure he paused to murmur:

'You've really, never—?'

'Could you leave now?' Veronica interrupted with clipped emphasis.

'Have none of your other lovers—?'

She lifted her chin. 'Will you please get out!'

She could feel his eyes running possessively over her body. 'Maybe they've just been incompetent, because you certainly liked it when *I*—'

'Would you just *go*!' she hastily cut him off before he started to brag. Men! When you wanted them to talk they were infuriatingly sullen and uncommunicative and when you wanted them to shut up they were relentless!

'OK, I'm going…but bear in mind I'm the boy next door,' he reminded her in a husky drawl that was like sandpaper against her frayed nerves. 'I can be over in a flash if you need me for any reason whatsoever…'

'I won't,' she bit out.

Her defiant certainty earned her a dark chuckle. 'Wait and see. The nights here are long and hot, especially if you have something on your mind that might make you feel restless and prone to feverish dreams. Feel free to come and get me if you're tossing and turning sleeplessly in your lonely bed tonight, and decide you want company for a midnight skinny-dip or an intimate friend to run a dripping wet ice cube over every delectable dip and hollow of your hot, naked body…'

And while she was coping with that highly disturbing image he archly informed her that his room was the one over the arched portico they had seen when they walked around by the pool, with a separate entrance up the stone stairway flanked with urns and discreetly placed solar lights.

'So you don't have to go tiptoeing in through the house peering into all of the bedrooms to find me,' he said silkily. 'Although, come to think of it, tiptoeing *out* of bedrooms is actually your specialty!'

She was annoyed with herself for letting him get the last word, but she was even more annoyed for allowing him to get under her skin to the extent that she spent a very sweaty, wakeful night, getting up several times to spray cold water on her skin and take a drink from the bottle in the fridge, longing to shed her sprigged cotton boxers and matching singlet top but unable to bring herself to sleep naked when *he* was crouched in the shadows of her subconscious, poised to pounce whenever she closed her eyes.

How smug he would be to know he had succeeded in

making her dream about him, she thought crankily as she showered away the stickiness of the endless night and shimmied into a short, floral-patterned sundress.

The clock-tower tolled a single bell for the half-hour and she decided that six-thirty was possibly a little early to stroll up to the village to buy croissants for her breakfast, so she made herself a cup of tea and drank it out on the patio as she brushed her newly washed hair, listening to the pigeons cooing in the trees, soaking up the gentle warmth of the early sun as it climbed into azure sky.

She debated sending another patient text question to Karen about her plans, even though it would still be the middle of the night on Grand Bahama Island, which was where she was headed last time they communicated. Since her island-hopping sister seemed to be permanently switched to answering-phone mode there was little point in planning a call around the six-hour time difference, and so far Veronica had had to be content with a few intermittent texts from Karen, largely featuring the word 'cool'.

Of course, once Karen got here Veronica wouldn't have to worry about Lucien. He wasn't likely to continue his private game of seduction when she had her sister around to act as a buffer.

He had already met Karen, but perhaps he had forgotten how very beautiful she was, thought Veronica broodingly as she deftly braided her hair into a neat French plait that would fit comfortably under her straw hat. Lucien would probably take one look at the two of them together and realise he was going after the wrong sister.

The idea made her chest tighten. She might try to dismiss his attentions as empty flattery in the pursuit of lecherous self-interest, but some kernel of hope inside her still sheltered the daring notion that he truly found something special about *her*…

She took her keys but she didn't need to unlock the gate

and realised why as she rounded the corner of the vineyard and saw Melanie and Sophie walking ahead of her, Sophie swinging a large woven basket.

Veronica increased her pace to catch up. 'Hi, are we both going to the same place?'

'We're going to the *boulangerie* to get our bread while Dad's making scrambled eggs for breakfast,' reported Sophie gravely.

'And Luc's gone on ahead to the *lavoir* by the village square to get our drinking water,' added Melanie, explaining that St Romain was one of the very rare local villages whose historic, spring-fed fountain with its stone clothes-washing trough provided safe drinking water from its horizontal spout. 'People come from miles around to fill up. Why pay for bottled spring water in the shop when you can get the pure stuff right from the source, absolutely free?'

Totting up the amount she had spent on keeping herself hydrated since she came to France, Veronica made a mental note to bring a couple of empty bottles next time she walked up to the town.

'You look a bit heavy-eyed. Did the morning bells wake you?' asked Melanie sympathetically. 'They used to chime through the night as well, but some newcomers to the village complained about the "noise pollution"—' she pulled a face to show she disapproved '—so after hundreds of years of happy tradition they now only ring the daylight hours. Mum used to say that one of the lovely things about coming here was that, day or night, she always knew the time without having to wear a watch.'

'I think I was awake well before the sun came up,' admitted Veronica, thinking of all the times in the night she had pored over the luminous dial of her watch, hoping to see that her ordeal was nearing an end.

'I know what *that's* like,' sighed Melanie, adjusting the set of her sling. 'I don't wear this in bed but if I lie the wrong way on my arm I feel like a knife is jabbing into me.' She frowned. 'I hope it wasn't because your bed was uncomfortable?'

'I think maybe I haven't quite recovered my sleep patterns after being sick in Paris,' said Veronica hurriedly, successfully diverting the older woman from the embarrassing reason for her sleeplessness.

Melanie instantly demanded the details and was aghast at her lonely suffering. 'Oh, you poor thing. You should have said something…perhaps you'd like to stay up at the Mas until you—'

'No, really—I'm fine now,' Veronica interrupted hastily. 'It's probably more the heat than anything else.'

'If you get hot in the night you should go for a swim in the pool,' said Sophie as they turned the corner to see the sign for the bakery at the top of the main street, next to the bell-tower archway that led to the St Romain Château, now a private medical clinic. 'That's what Luc does. He said he had a midnight swim last night.'

Ha! thought Veronica. She hoped it was a case of the biter bit.

'What did you think of Luc? Did he say anything to you when he walked to the car last evening?' Melanie startled her by asking.

'About what?' said Veronica cautiously.

'Oh, I don't know. I just wondered if he seemed all right to you. I never quite know where I am with Luc,' she confessed ruefully. 'It seems an awful thing to say but even as a child I found him a bit intimidating. Oh, not that he was a bully, or anything like that,' she said quickly, on seeing Veronica's stiffening expression. 'He was always quiet and polite, so much so it used to worry me. He had a genius IQ, you see, and seemed such a…*self-sufficient* little boy. He never seemed to really *need* me for anything, not the way my biological children did…'

Veronica tried to control her fascinated expression as

Melanie sketched a brief word-picture of young Lucien, born the son of Melanie's best friend, who had died in childbirth.

'Don and I got married straight away so he wouldn't lose custody of Luc—but we were really only friends, and a pretty ill-matched pair at that.' She laughed wryly. 'He was a motorcycle stunt rider, for goodness' sake! And no way was I ready to be a mother. I think we were both in a state of shock and thought we were doing the right thing for Lucien, but when it wore off we realised we were heading for disaster. The marriage didn't even last six months. Don kept custody of Lucien and moved to Australia, but when Luc was ten Don was killed in a motorcycle stunt and, since there were no other relatives, Miles and I agreed to take him in.'

They halted outside the narrow little shop and Sophie slipped in through the creaking screen door as Melanie wound up her brief story.

'We never regretted it, and I made sure he knew he was a welcome part of a loving family, but I always wondered whether I'd failed him as a baby by letting him go with his father, and I think that guilt made it difficult for me to push myself in where I was afraid he wouldn't want me to go…so I let him be too aloof, respected his privacy too much when I should just have waded in and smothered him with hugs and kisses whether he wanted them or not, as I did the others. Of course, the twins were toddlers then, and sucked up a lot of my energies, and I was starting to write, so Mum looked after Luc after school a lot of the time. If ever I mention it now, Luc claims that Don was a great dad and he was never aware of missing a mother when he was little, but he never could bring himself to call me anything but Melanie in the whole six years he lived with us, so I guess that tells me something. If anything, I think Mum is more of a mother-figure to him than *I* am. I've heard him call her Gran sometimes.' Melanie looked abashed as she heard her own words. 'Do I sound a little jealous? Maybe I am. Mum and he just seemed to click with each other from day one...'

'Perhaps being a grandmother-figure put her at a more comfortable emotional distance for him,' ventured Veronica. 'For a boy without a mother the whole concept might have been a bit overwhelming.'

Melanie's blue eyes lightened with the thought. 'You know, you just might be right.'

'You're not all that much older than he is, so perhaps he looks on you now as a sort of big sister rather than a step-mother,' Veronica added, holding the screen door open, her mouth watering as the sweet and savoury smells of hot bread and sugary spices wafted out to greet them.

She had spoken seriously but Melanie was still laughing about it when they stepped back out into the sunlight, Sophie's basket stacked with long loaves and sticky buns and Veronica clutching her bag of warm croissants.

'Oh, hello, Luc, we were just talking about you!'

Lucien shifted the armful of square plastic containers against his chest, revealing damp patches on the front of his tee shirt and jeans as he chopped back his stride to join their leisurely pace, walking on the cobbled road to leave the footpath free for the three females.

'Saying something nice, I hope,' he said, tilting his head in Veronica's direction as she ducked hastily to the far side of Sophie.

'Flattering to *me*, anyway,' smiled Melanie. 'Veronica thinks I'm young enough to be your sister.'

'Well, there're only two more years between you and I, than there are between me and Sophie,' he pointed out, with a gentle amusement that suggested to Veronica that she might have been right. She was jolted out of her complacency when he went on: 'What about your family, Veronica? How do you enjoy being a big sister?'

Lured into the conversation, she was forced to politely respond to his persistent queries until mention of Karen prompted Melanie to break in:

'What a pity she wasn't with you in Paris when you were so frightfully ill. Veronica was stranded in the apartment with a bad case of flu for most of her stay and missed out on a lot of what she wanted to see,' she told Luc, too absorbed in her own thoughts to see the snapping look he sent across to the other side of the footpath. 'Perhaps she can somehow add a few days onto the end of her holiday and go back and do all the things she'd planned. I don't think the apartment is booked up—I'll check on it for you, Veronica. Otherwise...perhaps...I thought she might stay at *your* place, Luc—?' she began diffidently.

Veronica could feel herself start to hyperventilate. 'Oh, no—'

'Why, yes, for some reason I can quite clearly picture her happily snuggling down there,' Luc overrode her spluttering protest with gloating smoothness.

'The poor thing had such a rotten start to her holiday that I'm determined to make it up to her.' Melanie was on an unstoppable roll now. 'I was going to get her to drive around and pick up samples and menus and product lists from some of the places in my research file which coincide with the markets that she'll find useful, but if she's doing the driving she won't be able to enjoy the scenery.' She paused expectantly and Veronica gritted her teeth as Luc obligingly met his cue.

'That's very true. You really want someone else behind the wheel...Ashley, or Ross perhaps?' he suggested helpfully.

'Lucien! You know Ashley is hopeless with a left-hand drive and she wouldn't be at all happy if we dragged Ross away from her side. Anyway, it should be someone who knows something about the area so Veronica won't have to bury her head in maps.'

'Mmm, I guess it'll have to be Miles, then.'

'Lucien!' Melanie halted at the corner where the footpath gave way to the stony grass verge beside the rows of vines, her frustration turning to the tug of a smile as she realised that his bland response to her heavy-handed hint was a tease. 'Miles is trying to get the new bathroom done by next week.' Lucien opened his mouth. 'And Mum is busy putting the garden to rights!' she added with a twinkle.

Veronica could only watch helplessly as her destiny was whisked out of her own hands by joint conspiracy.

'*I* could learn how to drive if someone could show me how.' Sophie had cleverly worked out the adult game and joined in, grinning as she broke off a crusty end of one of the bread sticks and stuffed it in her mouth. 'Luc could teach me. He's a really good driver.'

'Yes, I am, aren't I?' he said modestly. 'And I happen to have a rather classy convertible, which is perfect for zipping about the countryside scoping out the scenery. And nothing much to do but sit around and fret over my misfortunes.'

'So—this way we kill three birds with one stone. Well, that's settled, then!' beamed Melanie, wafting her swathed elbow like the wave of a magic wand.

Luc showed a rather terrifying affinity for reading minds as he directed a heavy-lidded look of searing amusement into appalled dove-grey eyes and declared softly:

'Veronica—you *shall* go to the ball…'

CHAPTER SIX

FOUR days later Veronica had realised that she had referenced the wrong fairy tale. She felt more like Sleeping Beauty than Cinderella, as her mind and body were slowly awakened to an enchanting new world of bewitching possibilities, horizons that were once limited to what was practicable, expanded to the limitless vista of *what if…*

Not that Lucien continued to put overt pressure on her to change her mind about him—he had been far too cunning for that. After his initial aggressive move he seemed prepared to laze in wait and let the sensuous allure of the time and the place and the extravagant beauty of her surroundings soak into Veronica's heart and soul, and undermine her efforts to maintain a polite standard of decorum. The landscape, which looked so harsh and stony at first sight, was astonishingly lush and verdant, and everywhere they went there were visions of bursting ripeness—from the heavily laden apricot trees they passed on the roads, the deep orange fruit clustered on the bowing branches, to the fields of corn and brilliant yellow sunflowers, their huge, flat faces turned to follow the path of their golden namesake across the azure sky, to the rows of glossy, brightly coloured fruits and vegetables temptingly laid out for display on the market tables.

Veronica had been seduced by Paris, but she quite simply

fell in love with Provence, and Lucien was right there beside her to assist her fall. Under the benign instructions of her well-meaning fairy godmother, he introduced her to a feast of the senses that she would have had to be a saint to resist.

Even in holy surroundings he seemed to find a way to lead her into temptation.

'Which ones do you like?'

Melanie's latest errand had sent them to an early morning farmer's market where Veronica had taken dozens of photographs and Luc picked up an order of thick-skinned dried sausages and olive oils, and then to the bookstore at the ancient Cistercian Abbey at Sénanque, a working monastery set amongst the blazing purple lavender fields in a remote valley high in the Vaucluse. They had already purchased the list of titles Melanie had asked for from the superb array of books about Provence food and customs and now Veronica had her nose pressed wistfully to the glass cabinet that displayed a range of religious souvenirs and crafts. She knew that *santons* were a famous product of Provence but she had never seen such fine examples.

'I can't decide. I love all of them.' She sighed, looking at the groupings of small, hand-painted terracotta figurines depicting various nativity scenes.

'Then why don't you buy them all?' murmured Luc, peering over her shoulder.

There spoke a millionaire!

'Because I can't afford to,' said Veronica wryly. 'But I am thinking that something like those packaged sets would look good in the Out Of The Box "Corporate Christmas" catalogue, although they might be a bit too expensive for bulk gifts—'

She broke off, biting her lip. She had tried to avoid talking directly about her company to Luc, conscious that he had suspected her of wanting free advice and determined to prove him wrong, but it was practically impossible to suppress her excitement when a great idea popped into her head or she saw something in a market that she was eager to add to her inventory.

'Not if you're interested in the top end of the market,' said Luc, leaning in for a closer look. 'These are obviously collector-quality, and don't forget you're looking at the retail price. You could make them small but exclusive private offerings to selected customers—that always goes down well. I can see company wives appreciating the unique character of a gift that could join the family Christmas heirlooms. If you played that angle up, the giving of additional pieces could even turn into an ongoing company tradition. And for non-Christian employees there are other *santonniers* who produce traditional secular characters representing different trades and crafts,' he finished shrewdly, giving her yet another glimpse of the forward-thinking that was the reason he *was* a millionaire.

She had already jotted down all the details she would need to investigate further, enabling her to justify the expense as she gave into the temptation of selecting a boxed set for herself—a small, stylised Mary and Joseph and a thumbnail-sized baby Jesus firmly tucked up in his white swaddling-cloth in the manger.

Luc watched with indulgent amusement as she made her careful choice, with a regretful glance at the shepherds and animals, all cast to the identical, modest scale of her selection, that the shop assistant was locking back up in the display cabinet.

'Don't worry, by next year you'll probably be so successful you'll be able to come back and buy the whole stable,' he said, and she hurried off to pay and bury her nose in a rack of calendars, turning her back on him to hide the absurd glow of pleasure at the implied praise in his throwaway remark.

They walked back to the car park past the rows of lavender, their spiky purple-topped stalks clotted with humming bees, and Luc paused to offload his paper carry-bags in the boot.

'Do you prefer it up or down?' he asked as they got into

the car, Veronica looked at him blankly for a moment before she realised he was talking about the convertible's hard-top.

'Oh...I don't mind—whatever you like,' she said, her diffidence not quite disguising her flustered thoughts, and he clicked his tongue.

'Tsk, tsk, Miss Veronica...what naughty thoughts are buzzing about in your brain?' he speculated wickedly, but fortunately the shadow of the canopy as it descended to snap into place threw a light veil across her pinkening cheeks as he twitched off her hat to throw it along with his into the rear jump seat.

'So much for your boasting about the charms of zipping about in your convertible,' she summoned the composure to taunt back as they drove along the narrow, winding road up through the rocky hills.

'Well, I enjoy the wind in my face, but there's a lot to be said for the sybaritic pleasures of air-conditioning when it's forty degrees outside,' he admitted as he dialled the internal temperature down to a delicious, skin-chilling coolness. He slanted her a brief look as he added blandly: 'Actually, like you, I enjoy it any which way...I think variety adds a certain piquancy to the experience,' he continued smoothly. 'But I never like to disappoint a lady, so I always offer her first choice.'

As usual she couldn't resist trying to puncture his masculine confidence. 'We *are* still talking about the car, aren't we?' she said primly.

'Of course, what else?' He grinned. 'Hungry yet?'

'Ravenous.' It had been several hours since her breakfast of fruit and croissants, and taste-testing at the market had only made her hungry for more. In spite of the heat, her appetite had increased markedly since she arrived. Flavours seemed more intense, the cooking fragrances more delicious, the wines headily infused with the very essence of summer.

'I'm glad I'm doing so much walking about—everything here is so scrumptious it's difficult to say no.' She sighed.

'We *are* still talking about food, aren't we?' deadpanned Luc, and Veronica could only laugh.

'Then we'll stop off for lunch at Gordes on the way back,' he decided, dismissing her half-hearted suggestion that Melanie would be expecting them back. By now the routine had been established—if any work had to be done it was done in the morning, the heat of the afternoon was time for siesta and the various members of the family to more or less please themselves where they went, only all coming together again in the evening for a leisurely alfresco dinner.

The day before, Veronica and Luc had lunched at a cheap market stall where delicious paella had been ladled out from a huge, simmering cauldron, and the day before that at an elegant, terraced restaurant high above the famous red ochre cliffs of Roussillon, where every dish had been a visual, as well as culinary, feast.

So today it was the little village perched on the crest of a rocky peak, stone houses and winding streets cascading down the hillside from the medieval château and church at the top. In the shady courtyard of a tiny restaurant protected by vine-covered stone walls, Veronica ate chicken roasted to melting tenderness in herbs and served on a little cake of smoothed lentils mixed with vegetables, and gorged herself on a luscious fig tart for dessert.

Mellowed by the food and wine, she stopped inspecting his every word and expression for ulterior meanings and allowed herself to be entertained by his scathing wit and far-ranging conversation, ever more intrigued by the complexities of his personality. In the mature man she could see the echoes of the orphan boy that Melanie had found so disconcerting, his free-wheeling mind constantly absorbed by new ideas and challenges, his emotional detachment most obvious when his intellect was fully engaged. Yet he also possessed a deeply sensual side to his nature with which he seemed equally at ease.

Later that afternoon, Veronica was floating dreamily on her back in the swimming pool, spread-eagled arms gently paddling to keep herself afloat, the sun burning hot against her closed eyelids as she continued to ponder the fascinating contradictions in Luc Ryder's character.

A loud splash invaded her drifting consciousness, destroying the serenity of the pool and causing her limbs to flail as she tried to keep herself afloat on the suddenly choppy surface of the water. At first she thought it must be Sophie doing one of her forbidden 'bombs', but as she coughed up a mouthful of water and blinked away the blurry beading along her eyelashes she caught sight of a male body shooting past her under the water.

Instant exhilaration charged through her veins and she jackknifed upright, planting her feet firmly astride on the bottom of the chest-deep pool to brave the slapping waves, sweeping the water from her hair and face as she turned to face the invader. In spite of Melanie's open invitation she had tried to avoid coming down to the pool when she knew the adult members of the family were using it, several times having backed off after glimpsing Luc cutting smoothly through the water on a seemingly endless series of laps, barely creating a ripple with his streamlined stroke.

Expecting a sleek, seal-dark head to break the water after the dive, followed by a pair of lean, tawny shoulders, she felt a stab of disappointment as she saw Ross Bentley's chiselled features bob up at the far end of the pool. To her dismay he flashed a smile at her expectant face and began to swim back towards her, head down, his solid arms and legs attacking the water with more aggression than grace.

Uncaring that it might seem rude, Veronica headed for the wide, curving stairs at the near end of the pool, but before she could get there Ross circled around in front of her, one hand reaching up to grip the tiled edge of the pool and pull himself upright, barring her way with his thick body, bronzed to an unlikely tan by the exclusive Melbourne sun-bed clinic Ashley had boasted they had both attended to prepare for the holiday.

'What's your hurry?' he said, with a smug grin. 'I saw you swimming earlier—you're not too bad, for a woman. What say we have a race? I was a surf life-saving champ for years, so to make it fair I'll let you have a good head start.'

He managed to incorporate some reference to his own superior attributes into almost every statement he made, thought Veronica, aware that to argue would invite more of his unwanted attention. She had offended his ego by ignoring him at their first meeting and he was determined to make her regret it, but she was extremely wary of his over-friendliness and constant preening, sensing that it was less to do with her than with his competitive need to assert his masculinity in front of an Alpha male. Unfortunately, he had all of Luc's arrogance but none of his insight or critical self-awareness, and his inability to laugh at himself was a serious handicap to his charm.

On the second night of her stay, Veronica had allowed herself to be gently bullied into having dinner with the Reeds when they had some friends over, thinking it would give her the excuse to politely refuse future invitations. The extra company of strangers had provided some welcome camouflage, but she had spent an uncomfortable part of the evening trying to steer clear of Ross's roving eyes and hands, and since then had taken care not to be left alone with him.

Now she was in precisely the kind of situation she had tried to avoid. Clad only in a skimpy, halter-necked tankini, she was acutely aware of her vulnerability.

'I think I've been in long enough already—my skin is starting to get waterlogged.' She laughed lightly to cover her unease, lifting a hand out of the water to waggle her slightly wrinkled fingers at him.

He grabbed her wrist, holding it playfully tight as he crabbed closer. 'Oh, c'mon, you don't really want to get out,' he told her confidently. 'Didn't I see you playing pool tag yesterday with Sophie—how about a game of that with me?'

'Sounds a bit too strenuous right now,' she responded, her skin crawling at the thought. 'I only came in to cool off. Um, where's Ashley?' she asked brightly, looking hopefully past him to the pathway that led from the house.

Her heart sank when his beefy, wet shoulders shrugged. 'Who knows? She's in one of her pets because it was her turn to help Zoe around the house.' His mouth twisted in derision. 'Can you believe that even after what happened to Melanie they don't have a full-time housekeeper, just a cleaner who comes in a couple of times a week?'

'Well, this is a family holiday home, not a full-service hotel,' Veronica pointed out, using the distraction to twist her arm so that it slid out of his wet grasp. 'Enjoy your swim!' she added, attempting to dive around him without waiting for a reply.

But her triumphant relief was short-lived when he threw his body sideways so that she bumped into him, laughing as she surfaced, spluttering.

'I thought you didn't want to play,' he said, starting to rough-house in earnest, taking an almost sadistic pleasure in the unevenness of the contest, his legs tangling with hers as his hands tried to drag her under.

'I *don't*—' she said, threshing away from him, the back of her neck hitting the tiled edge of the pool, too intent on her furious defence to notice Sophie briefly appear from between the flowering oleanders and drop her towel as she turned to race back towards the house. 'Go and find Ashley if you want a playmate—'

'Aw, don't be like that!' He chased after her, still laughing, caging her with both arms against the plastered side of the pool. 'You looked bored floating around by yourself. I just thought a big girl like you might be up for a little bit of fun—'

'Not with *you*—' Too late she realised the revulsion that had leaked into her voice was a direct attack on his vanity.

His laughter congealed into an ugly grin. 'You suddenly got something better to do? Or should I say some*one*? You looked keen enough when you saw me dive in. Maybe you thought I was lover-boy—'

Something must have flickered in her eyes because his expression turned malicious as he realised his random spite had hit a mark. 'You did!' he crowed, thrusting his face aggressively towards hers to jeer: 'You can stop acting holier than thou about Ashley and me if that's what you're up to. But you're kidding yourself if you think a freckle-faced hick like you is anything special to *him*. He's had more beautiful women than you've had hot dinners. Your sister, for one—'

Veronica went rigid. 'That's not true!'

'Oh, yeah? Ask Ash! Melanie emailed her some pictures on their last visit to London, and they show Karen draped all over Ryder at some fancy dinner he took them to… You're not going to tell me a guy like him is going to turn down a looker like your sister when she climbs into his lap to play kissy-face—'

'It really isn't any of my business,' she said through stiff lips, but Ross had scented blood in the water and ripped into her with a shark-like tenacity.

'It is if he's trying to get into your pants as well,' he snickered. 'Maybe he gets a kick out of doing sisters. And then there's that hot-and-heavy *ménage à trois* he's got going in London that we're all supposed to ignore. I don't suppose he's dished up all the dirty details to you about *that*…' His sneering contempt was mixed with undercurrents of lustful envy.

It took all her control to maintain her frigid front. 'I have no idea what you're talking about.'

But her coolness only goaded him to greater excess. 'If he's such a hot stud you'd think that he wouldn't have to sniff around after other men's wives…or run away like a snivelling coward when he got caught, instead of standing up for himself like a *real* man—'

Veronica had had enough. He thought he could smear her with his vile thoughts with impunity, because she would be too ashamed to repeat them. Perhaps he was right, but that didn't mean she had to meekly listen to his abuse.

She went to duck under one of his arms, only to have him lower it and say with nauseating menace, 'Where do you think you're going, honey?'

She was debating how effective a sharp knee in the groin would be, fearing the water resistance would be too great to land a telling blow, when she heard the slap of feet on the paving.

She looked up to see Luc and Sophie walking around the pool towards them, Sophie pink and slightly breathless in her bright blue swimsuit, Luc in cut-off jeans, shedding his patterned shirt and sunglasses onto one of the stone benches, revealing a sweaty torso and dust streaks on his face as he took a flat, shallow dive directly over their heads, arrowing to the other side and back under the water before popping up beside them with a lazy smile.

'Hi, you two. What's going on?'

'Nothing much,' said Ross, who had hastily dropped both arms as soon as Luc had hit the water. For all his cast-iron confidence his grin was a trifle nervous, although he must have known that he wasn't about to be contradicted. 'Veronica and I were just talking about having a race. I was offering to give her a head start.'

'That's not much of a challenge, old man,' said Luc, casting Veronica a disparaging look that normally would have made her bristle. However she was too relieved by his miraculous appearance to do anything but cling gratefully to the side of the pool as he directed his dark-eyed gaze back to Ross.

'You were a life-saving champ a few years ago, weren't you? You're probably used to the action being fast and furious,' he said with a man-to-man respect that made Ross's grin widen, his tension easing. Luc executed a watery somersault and stroked over to scoop up the ball that was sitting by the pool skimmer, swimming back with it spinning on his upraised finger.

'So why don't the two of us play some one-on-one instead—no complicated rules, just first one with ten goals in the opposition net wins,' he said easily.

'Hey, Soph!' He raised his voice to call to the little girl who had sat on the edge of the pool, her legs dangling in the water alongside Veronica. 'Will you get those floating baskets from the pool locker and hook them at the ends of the pool? Ross and I are going to have a game. That's if you're not afraid of going mano-a-mano,' he added in a tone of voice calculated to produce the exact effect that it did. 'Are you up for it, or not?'

Ross lunged through the water to snatch away the ball. 'Bring it on!'

What was brought on was a quick, brutal, no-holds-barred confrontation, which ended with Luc scoring his tenth easy goal to Ross's hard-won five. Veronica had edged around to sit on the steps with Sophie, out of the way of the explosive splashes and leaping collisions, slightly stunned by the grim intensity with which both men played. Although Luc didn't have Ross's chunky slabs of gym-sculpted muscle, his lean proportions gave him a better power-to-weight ratio, his lithe speed and supple flexibility enabling him to manoeuvre so quickly he often left his increasingly desperate opponent wallowing in his wake. In fact, Veronica judged that it would have been a complete annihilation except for the fact that Luc seemed to tire abruptly towards the end, allowing Ross to score all of his goals in the last few minutes of the contest.

Ross, of course, immediately proposed a best-of-three, but Luc had already swung himself out of the side of the pool and was sliding his feet into his shoes and thrusting his wet arms into his shirt, squeezing the water out of his sodden pony-tail and briskly rebanding it.

'No, thanks, I've just been digging up a new area of vege garden for Zoe. I think I've had enough exercise for one day,' he said, dropping his sunglasses into his chest pocket. 'Good game, though,' he added laconically and Veronica noticed that unlike Ross, who was wheezing heavily, he barely seemed out of breath.

He padded around to unhook a netted hoop and Veronica swam over to get the one from the shallow end, handing it up to him, trying not to notice the way the soaking denim clung to his thighs as he crouched and then stood to hand them to Sophie, who trotted away to drop them back in the locker.

He looked down at her. 'Had enough?' he demanded, flicking a glance at Ross, who was still trying to recover his breath, and Veronica realised that beneath his cool front was a banked fury.

She nodded hastily, but before she could turn back to the steps Luc bent, extending his hands, and when she tentatively placed her own in his, he pulled her out of the pool in a single movement, as if she weighed less than a feather, a brief ripple of contraction across the hard abdomen bared by his open shirt the only sign of effort. At close quarters she could feel the full impact of his angry tension.

He stepped back and gave her wet swimsuit a raking look that made her conscious of the high-cut briefs that extended her already long legs and the deep cleavage of the ruched halter top that was designed to support her full breasts, moulding them high against her chest, the double lining not thick enough to hide the outline of her nipples, pebbled by the cool water.

'Is this yours?' He moved over to pick up the large striped towel that lay across one of the sunloungers, and when she nodded he shook it out and held it up.

Veronica walked nervously towards him, far too aware of her body. He made her conscious of her essential femininity in a way that Ross's suggestive leering never could, but she sensed he was in a dangerous mood.

His brown eyes were a fathomless black that made her skin goose-pimple as he dropped the towel over her shoulders, and she quickly wrapped it, sarong-like, around her body.

She didn't dare object as he escorted her up the path and was relieved when Sophie ran up between them.

'Luc's driving Gran and me over to St Didier soon, to see the Jarditrain, and we wondered if you wanted to come?' she said. 'It's a huge model railway this man has built in his back garden, with twenty-five different trains that run all around the track, through all sorts of scenery and tunnels and over bridges and stuff like that...'

'Sounds fun,' said Veronica distractedly, and stumbled over an uneven joint in the pavestones as Luc said:

'Why don't you run along and get changed, Sophie, while I make sure Veronica is OK?'

'Oh, sure...' Sophie paused and turned big eyes up to Veronica. 'I wasn't sure what to do, but Luc always knows,' she said in a matter-of-fact voice. 'He told me once when I was being bullied at school that if you're not big enough to beat someone yourself you have to find someone to be your champion.'

'Sophie didn't know what you and Ross were doing, but she thought you looked upset, so she ran to get me,' clipped Luc as the girl peeled off towards the house, pigtails bouncing. 'You're damned lucky she decided to look for you at the pool, and that I was working out in the garden. Unless we misread the situation and you were enjoying what he was doing—'

'Of course I wasn't!' Veronica denied fiercely, still feeling shaken by the whole ugly incident. In hindsight it was obvious that Luc and Sophie hadn't simply wandered onto the scene by chance. 'I know I have to thank you for distracting him—'

'Don't thank me yet,' he muttered grimly, lengthening his stride as they passed under the twin almond trees at the edge of the cottage garden.

'I'm glad you won when you did,' she said, wary of his meaning as she hurried to keep up with him. 'He was scoring so well there at the end I was afraid—'

He halted her with a blistering look. 'Only because I let him,' he bit out. 'Ten-zip would have been more gratifying for me, but it would have been counter-productive. When you beat a man that completely, you don't humiliate him as well— unless you want to make a bad enemy,' he said, stepping back to let her precede him into the cottage. 'I may happen to think Bentley's a pompous bastard with an over-inflated opinion of his self-worth, but he's Ashley's fiancé, so a certain amount of diplomacy is required in getting the message across…'

'What message?' she asked, nervously hugging the towel around her.

'That you're under my protection,' he replied, his voice redolent with dark satisfaction.

Her face registered her instinctive objection to the implication and he was swift to strike.

'You want me to tell him you're *not*?' he invited with dangerous softness.

The consequences of that didn't bear thinking about. She swallowed. 'I'm sure he won't try anything like that again—'

'Did he say that?'

'Well, no, but—'

'But what? Did he have reason to think you wanted him to try it on with you? Did you and he *arrange* to sneak off for a watery rendezvous—'

'Don't be ridiculous. I think he's repulsive!' she snapped.

'Then what in the *hell* did you think you were doing in the pool with him?' His rage broke loose in a low roar. 'Damn it, don't tell me you don't know what a lecher he is. I've seen the way he leers over you when Ashley's not around. Why the hell did you let him get close enough to grab you—?'

'I didn't *let* him do anything,' she protested, buffeted by his unleashed fury, trying to persuade herself that his anger wasn't really directed at her.

His brown eyes smouldered with hostility. 'You shouldn't have gone down to the pool alone.'

She blinked, rocked by the accusation. 'Are you blaming *me*?'

'At the very least you could have got out as soon as you saw him coming—'

'I didn't *see* him coming, that was the problem.' It was her turn to blister him with a look. 'You *are* blaming me,' she said incredulously.

His olive skin darkened and he shifted his feet. 'That swimsuit fits you like a second skin,' he muttered.

Her eyes widened. 'That's because it's designed for *swimming*,' she pointed out sarcastically. 'Do you expect me to wear my clothes when I go into the pool? How dare you try and blame me for Ross's behaviour? His lack of self-control is his own problem, not mine!' She stepped up to poke him in the chest with an outraged finger as she spoke. 'He wanted to play a game of tag, obviously as an excuse to feel me up, and I said no. How much clearer could I have been? I never invited him to touch me and I never will. Believe me, Ashley is welcome to the puffed-up sleazebag.' She ripped off her towel and threw it at him. 'I won't apologise for looking like this. Just because I slept *once* with you does not make me a slut!' she articulated starkly.

Streaks of colour mounted his hard cheekbones as his hand fisted in the damp towel. 'I never thought you were,' he said through clenched teeth. 'I'm not that much of a hypocrite—'

'You virtually accused me of making it easy for him!' she cried.

'I didn't say that. It's him I don't trust. I don't want him any-where near you,' he said with sullen belligerence. 'I don't like him touching you. I don't like the way he looks at you. He's damned lucky I only gave him a few unfriendly taps. If he does it again he won't be coming up for air again quite so quickly.'

Remembering the flying elbows, head-dunkings and jarring full-body smashes during the lawless one-on-one, Veronica marvelled at his understatement.

Then his words fully sank in and a possible source of his indiscriminate rage suddenly hit her between the eyes.

Her stomach flipped.

Was Luc *jealous*?

He was certainly acting like the quintessential territorial male, radiating a violent antagonism that signalled his domi-nance to challenger and female alike.

Or, given his murky recent past, was he just being dog in the manger?

She wished she hadn't made her dramatic gesture with the towel. Now she had nothing to hide behind. Except words. She stood straight and proud.

'I'm sure he won't. After all, he's already warned me against trusting *you*—'

He glowered. 'What's that supposed to mean?'

She couldn't back down now. The festering wound would never heal if she ignored it. 'He told me about you and Karen. He said you were more than just acquaintances—'

'And you *believed* him?' His thick fury almost convinced her, but she had seen the tell-tale shutters go up at the mention of her sister's name. 'He lives in Australia, for God's sake. What the hell would *he* know?'

'He said Ashley had photos of you and Karen at a dinner—'

'A *dinner*?' he interrupted scathingly. 'Is *that* all? No porno pics of us actually getting down and dirty, then?' he lashed out, his words dripping with acid. 'For God's sake, how could you give credence to *any*thing that cretin says? You said yourself he's a sleazebag! The only way he can make himself look good is to make someone else look bad!'

She knew he was right, but she also knew that lies were often based in truth, and trust was a two-way street.

'There's no smoke without fire.'

The trite phrase seemed to be the last straw. 'Well, if you'd rather believe him than me, go ahead!' he exploded. 'Unlike you I don't choose to run my life guided by the opinions of muckraking slime!'

He stormed out the door, leaving Veronica's head ringing as if she had been hit by a stun-grenade. He had never actually addressed the allegation at all, she thought numbly. Instead, all his anger had been directed at the fact that she had taken Ross's word as gospel.

But she hadn't...not really. Her own self-doubt had made the idea seem all too credible, but, still, she had harboured the secret expectation that Luc would flatly deny the accusation as a slanderous lie. If he had, she would have believed him in a heartbeat.

That he hadn't was a sickening blow to her unacknowledged feelings, leaving her fiercely grateful that she had fought the powerful attraction that had tempted her to abandon her pride and her principles to a transient affair.

CHAPTER SEVEN

FORCING herself into motion, Veronica walked into the bedroom, her mind a blessed blank as she undid the ties at the nape of her neck and peeled the clinging-wet bathing-top over her head, dropping it carelessly on the tiled floor beside the bed on the far side of the room. She frowned as she looked around, blinking an annoying blur from her eyes.

'Looking for this?'

Veronica spun around, rubbing fiercely at her wet lashes.

Luc came into focus as he stepped into the room, holding up her towel. 'Sorry, I forgot I was carrying it when I flounced off.' He smiled crookedly. 'I thought you might need it.'

With a gasp Veronica snatched up the nearest thing from the bed to cover her swaying breasts. Unfortunately it turned out to be a small, decorative cushion barely equal to the task. She hugged it to her chest with both arms.

His eyes didn't waver from her pale face and suspiciously bright eyes, his smile fading. 'I'm a little touchy on the subject of personal loyalty right now,' he said more sombrely. 'I'm afraid I was making you pay for someone else's sins. In the circumstances you had every right to ask what you did—and expect a straight answer, even if it's not a very edifying one. Sometimes a kiss is nothing more or less than a kiss.'

'W-what?'

'I'm talking about Karen,' he said abruptly. 'That public dinner just after they first came to London was the only time I ever kissed her, although, strictly speaking, Karen was the one doing the kissing. She'd had a few drinks too many and started throwing herself at me. Melanie was embarrassed, so I acted amused, and played along, trying to keep the flirtation light to avoid creating an awkward scene at the table, but Karen took it for encouragement. She developed a bit of a crush on me for a few weeks afterwards—kept ringing me, turning up at my office or on my doorstep, that kind of thing. She made a nuisance of herself until I asked Melanie to have a quiet word with her. I haven't seen her since.'

'Oh…' The stinging at the back of Veronica's eyes eased, but now her throat was too thickly clogged to speak. It sounded just like one of Karen's fleeting infatuations. In addition to her regular string of boyfriends, she had a habit of embarking on short-lived fixations with men who were either glamorously unattainable or potentially useful. Luc had probably qualified on both accounts.

'She's a very pretty girl but not my type at all,' Luc continued, prowling slowly around the end of the other bed. 'She seemed to think I would find her gorgeous self impossible to refuse but—unbelievable as it might be to both her and you— I was never even tempted to take her up on her invitation…'

Now he was closer, she realised he wasn't quite as subdued as he appeared. Even in wet cut-offs and a damp, unbuttoned shirt he exuded an air of panache, but beneath his civilised expression lurked a potent hint of untamed wildness. 'I don't find it unbelievable, Luc,' she admitted, 'I know what Karen can be like, you don't have to—'

'I find that my being rich is like an aphrodisiac to some women,' he confided softly, coming to a stop in front of her, making the wide space between the beds suddenly feel much more confining. 'They think that because I can have anything

I want, I automatically want to have everything. It doesn't occur to them that wealth enables me to be more—not less—discriminating. Or that I might not appreciate being objectified as some kind of sexual luxury-item for status-hunting females. That's why I steer clear of the usual fashionable haunts for the polished horde.'

He looked at her through a thick veil of lashes. 'You know, just because I slept with you in Paris doesn't mean I'm a promiscuous satyr…'

The breath whooshed out of her lungs and she could feel herself blushing from her head to her heels at the sly paraphrase of her own words. 'I'm sorry—' She bit down hard on her tongue. He had her so tangled up that *she* was now apologising to *him*!

'I'm not normally so reckless a lover,' he murmured. 'I stay away from casual pick-ups and I'm usually extremely careful about who I invite into my life. I truly do appreciate the rarity value of a woman like you…'

His lashes swept up as he trailed off to watch her nibble at the tantalising bait.

'L-like me?'

'A woman who's smart and not afraid to be herself, who takes responsibility for her own actions and stands up for her convictions…' He walked his fingers lightly up the side of her arm to the accompaniment of his words. 'A woman who has a good sense of humour, who's compassionate, and tolerant of other people's very human failings…'

She eyed him suspiciously as he toyed with the piped edge of the cushion that peeped out from under her protectively clamped elbows, and continued his flattering paean:

'A woman who's warm, generous and forgiving…' her eyes narrowed and his buttery voice slowed to a sexy drawl '…and deeply passionate…'

He gave the cushion a sharp tug that slid it out from beneath her folded arms. 'You're getting this all wet. Let me dry you properly,' he chided, throwing it out of reach on the other side of the bed and quickly moving in with the towel to dab at the beads of moisture dripping from her hair onto her shoulders, stroking the soft cotton down her breastbone, insinuating between her shielding hands.

'I can do that—' she said weakly.

'But I *want* to,' he insisted with implacable softness, brushing away her increasingly feeble attempts at concealment, and blotting over the creamy globes of her breasts with dedicated attention to detail. 'We don't want you catching a chill.'

'It's at least thirty-eight degrees outside,' Veronica raggedly protested the absurdity, shivering as the towel dragged across a tender nipple.

'But you're shivering,' he pointed out, gently frictioning her other nipple to a tingling point.

'Not from cold,' she choked, and his nostrils flared triumphantly at the heady scent of her swift arousal.

'Oh, I missed a bit,' he murmured, dropping the pretence of the towel altogether and bending his head to sip at a little droplet running down over the rounded side of her breast, lapping it up with a long stroke of his tongue, catching her by the waist as she shied, so that he could scrape his exquisitely rough jaw against her soft flesh and nuzzle his way to the quickening peak. Capturing the quivering bud between his firm lips, he began to suckle warmly, his other hand moving to cup the neglected breast and fondle it to a similar, aching fullness.

'Luc—' Her hands pressed against his slick chest, slipping against his damp skin.

'You can dry me next,' he promised, releasing his glistening captive for appreciative study before cherishing a series of softly exploring kisses to the tip of her left breast.

'I can see your heart beating,' he husked as he licked at the rhythmically pulsing nipple. 'Do I make your heart beat a little faster, Veronica?' he murmured, and took it deeply in his mouth, his hand sliding over the smooth fabric front of her high-cut briefs to run a finger back and forth over the pouting cleft at the juncture of her thighs, delicately tracing the puffy contours. 'How much faster can I make it go…?' he wondered as he rolled his hot, wet tongue around her nipple and pressed it against the slick hardness of the roof of his mouth as he suckled more strongly, sinking his teeth deep into her sensitised flesh.

Her shuddering body arched helplessly and he lifted his head, his arm going around her supple waist as he teased out her pleasure with skilful fingers, increasing the wringing dampness of the taut fabric pulled tight between her legs.

'You can thank me now,' he growled, looking down into her passion-hazed face with heavy-lidded satisfaction.

'I—W-what—?' she panted, struggling for oxygen to fuel the wild-fire in her blood.

'You wanted to thank me for providing a distraction in the pool. I wasn't ready to be thanked then. I am now,' he told her silkily. 'After all, I gained quite a lot of scrapes and bruises acting as your champion.'

'Quite a few of those were your own account.' Her hands tightened on his muscled shoulders, her nails digging into his skin to punish him for his taunting delay. 'You *enjoyed* making it brutal.'

'It could have been Ashley who blundered in on you. I did rescue you from that embarrassment,' he said, taking a little nip of her lower lip.

'You're determined to be a hero, aren't you?' she said breathlessly.

'As long as I get a hero's reward,' he growled, and took her mouth in a savage kiss, dragging her breasts against his chest, making her utter a muffled cry of pain as one of the buttons on his shirt caught against her turgid nipple.

He wrenched his mouth from hers. 'What's the matter?' He gripped her arms, holding her scantily clad body away to inspect it for evidence of harm. 'Damn it, if that bastard hurt you...'

She could have screamed with disappointment. 'It was just your shirt button,' she said, furious with herself for breaking the mood.

To her frustration Luc seemed reluctant to take her word for it. His jaw clenched as his eyes burned over her. 'He had you pushed against the wall when I arrived—'

'Really, I'm OK. He got in a few sly gropes, that's all. That's probably all he intended to do so he could laugh it off as accidental, but he lost his temper when I said no—'

'He's the type who likes forbidden fruit,' he brooded.

'Don't we all,' she said shakily, suddenly thinking of some of the other sleazy things that Ross had said. Given his penchant for distorted fact and jealous fiction, should she give any credence at all to his vicious words? Or should she rely on her instincts, and wait for Luc to trust her enough to bring up the subject himself?

She shifted restlessly in his hold, remembering his words about her paying for someone else's sins. Did she really want to get involved if he was on the rebound from some disastrous entanglement? Or worse?

'He's envious of you,' she said. 'He wants to be like you, but he knows he can never match up.'

His bitter-chocolate eyes melted to a glossy, dark smile of sultry intent. 'I'm glad you think so.' His hands slid to her hips and slowly moved her back against him.

She splayed her hands against his chest and tipped her head back to focus on his face. 'Because a man who thinks it's OK to cheat on his commitment to a woman is likely to cheat in other ways, too...'

'I agree,' he murmured, pressing his mouth to a teasing freckle at the side of her mouth. 'With me it's either all—' he steadily pushed his hard thigh between her bare legs, lifting it to ride tightly against her feminine dampness '—or nothing…' He slowly withdrew it again, and snuggled her against his chest and hips, his hands roaming her long, naked back, moulding her pliant body to the straining contours of rigid muscle.

'So tell me you want it all, Veronica…' he invited in a velvety-dark tone, gathering her between his spread thighs, and shifting her so that her back was to the bed. 'And let me show you that what happened in Paris was only a tiny taste of what we can give each other…'

It was an answer of sorts, she persuaded herself, giving up to the delicious falling sensation and giving a little squeak when it proved to be real and her back landed with a bounce on the mattress.

He laughed as he followed her down, his hand moving to the centre of his body. She heard the metallic slide of a zip, and at the same time a tapping at the front door, and a high, treble voice.

'Veronica? Are you there? Gran says she's just about ready to go to the Jarditrain.'

Luc slumped for a brief second on top of her, his full weight pressing her into the covers, his dark head buried between her lush breasts, then with a virulent curse under his breath he rolled off the bed and stood rigidly, his face twisting in a wry grimace as he eased himself uncomfortably back into the clammy denim and, with great difficulty, drew up the zip.

He looked at her, lying dazed on the bed, and leaned over to give her a deep-mouthed, possessive kiss. 'Hold that thought for tonight, *chérie*!' he whispered roughly, and strode out the door.

'Give her a few minutes, Soph. You know what women are like about their hair,' she heard him say coolly as he stepped outside. Moving away down the path, he added in a raised voice, clearly intended for her ears: 'If she's not down by the car in fifteen minutes we'll both come back and fetch her.'

In the event, Miles came with them too, confessing an interest in model railways that had been sadly thwarted by Luc and Justin both exhibiting boyhood preferences for building with Lego or constructing model cars rather than messing about with trains. Luc, Veronica learned, had built working miniature robots from scratch when he was twelve and sold them to his friends, starting a rage for robot battles that had spread through the neighbourhood and then the school like wildfire.

'The more robots that were destroyed by the fighting, the better for my profits. I was a stark-raving little capitalist even then,' he admitted as they bought their tickets at the gate.

'He sold his idea to a toy company and put the money away for his education,' revealed Zoe. 'By the time he got to Oxford he had more than enough to pay all the expenses that weren't covered by his scholarship and have seed money for his investments.'

'I also had Dad's life insurance money, which you were supposed to put towards my keep,' he said to Miles, his respect and affection for the man who had a hand in bringing him up very obvious.

Miles clapped him on the shoulder. 'If we'd charged all our kids for their upbringing we'd be richer than you right now.' He laughed. 'You were the least expensive of the lot! He was always too busy studying to bother about anything but books and his computer, which he mostly built himself,' he told Veronica. 'The lad had very spartan tastes.'

She flicked a startled glance at Luc, trying to visualise the ardent sensualist she knew as an ascetic.

'I would have become a monk,' he said blandly, 'but I do require a modicum of luxury in my life. I found I couldn't hack the rules about celibacy.'

'What's sella-bussy?' asked Sophie, who was following the adult conversation with her usual alertness.

Luc opened his mouth, but Zoe was too quick for him.

'Never getting married,' she said. 'Or engaged,' she tacked on, thinking she had covered the field

'Luc's not married or engaged,' Sophie instantly responded.

'Or ever having any girlfriends,' added Zoe firmly.

Sophie looked at Luc and covered her mouth, a giggle escaping between her fingers. He grinned back and waved an admonishing finger at her knowing face.

Along with their tickets they were given a list of objects to spot amongst the miniature landscape of villages, farms, mountains, bridges and rivers and an hilarious competition ensued, with Sophie proclaimed the final victor when she realised that the eagle no one could find was part of a carved Indian totem pole.

'How come *you* didn't win?' she demanded suspiciously of Luc, who had come in a narrow second.

'I would have, but Veronica kept distracting me,' he claimed. 'I think you two were secretly working together.'

Sophie pursed her lip, eyeing Veronica's flushed face. 'Are you sure I won fair and square?'

Luc ticked off his fingers. 'Your dad was too busy watching the "making of" film to find anything but the obvious, your gran skived off on the bench under the tree, Veronica kept being entranced by the trains and sneaking around trying to figure out what I was looking at and I was having too much fun misleading her to pay proper attention to what I was doing. Dedication and application, Sophie, that's what made you the winner.'

'All right!' Assured that she had justly earned her triumph, Sophie did her little dance of victory.

To celebrate her success, on the way home they stopped off at the café opposite the *lavoir* in St Romain and Miles bought them all lavish ice-cream concoctions, which they ate at one of the outside tables, under the spreading shade of a massive plane tree.

The conversation turned from the scale models they had seen to computer modelling and animation, specifically an animation feature film that had recently won an award, and Veronica discovered that Luc not only provided investment finance for businesses, he had also acted as Angel for a string of successful stage plays, musicals and independent films, anonymously backing the productions for a share of the profits.

'He knows heaps of famous film stars,' said Sophie, licking chocolate sauce off her spoon.

'I know *of* them,' he said drily. 'I make my money off the back-end of the production. I deal with accountants and producers, and sometimes directors. Apart from the occasional handshake introduction, I generally try to steer clear of all the publicity hoopla.'

'But you did say you'd take me to watch a film being made when I come to visit you in England,' Sophie reminded him. 'And maybe even to a première.'

He grinned at her awed tone. Veronica noticed that he never got annoyed with the girl's interruptions or innocently awkward questions or comments on subjects he might well prefer to avoid.

'Only if it's got a PG rating. We can't have you walking the red carpet only to have the door shut in your face and me dragged off in handcuffs for trying to corrupt a minor.'

'Then we'd appear on the Entertainment News Channel!' she said brightly, as if that would be the pinnacle of his achievements.

'Will no one rid me of this turbulent child?' he implored the heavens, thumping his fist on his heart.

Even Sophie, who didn't understand the historical allusion, burst out laughing at his dramatic declamation.

'Perhaps you should act in films yourself,' said Veronica. 'Though your florid style seems more suited to the silent era.'

He twirled an imaginary moustache over the top of a wicked leer. 'As a hero or villain?'

She hesitated, swallowing a mouthful of heavenly honey-and-almond ice cream, and he propped his chin on his hand, studying her across the tabletop. 'Still undecided, Veronica?' he challenged with a lazy amusement, his voice dropping to a provocative drawl. 'Maybe you'd like me to do another personal audition for you?'

Conscious of their audience, Veronica squinted at him in silent condemnation.

'Perhaps she realises you're clever enough to play either role effectively, if you set your mind to it,' said Zoe, picking up on the undertones that had Miles looking faintly baffled. 'You know what Napoleon said: put a rogue in the limelight and he'll act like an honest man. Well, *I* say put an honest man in the limelight and sometimes he'll act like a rogue.'

'Are you calling me a rogue, Zoe?' Luc appeared entertained rather than offended.

'I'm saying no man is completely one thing or the other, and a woman would be a fool to forget it,' she said stoutly. 'Fred was a wonderful person, but he drove like a maniac and was stubborn as a mule. He'd be alive today if he'd done what the doctor told him. Now sit up straight and let the girl finish her ice cream before it melts.'

'Yes, ma'am!'

When they got back to Mas de Bonnard, Melanie was pecking one-handedly at her laptop on the dining-room table, but she waved away Veronica's tentative offer of help, saying that she was just answering a few private emails.

'Thanks to you I've got plenty of reading and sorting to be getting on with, and Luc has downloaded some voice-recognition software for me so I'll be able to dictate my notes and ideas directly onto the computer so—panic over.' She smiled, after she had listened to Sophie's excited report and sent her off to wash her sticky face and hands.

'Which is fortunate as things are turning out—' She broke off, hitting the key that would send off her emails. 'Did Karen finally get through to you, by the way?' she said, swivelling in her seat. 'She rang here saying she'd been calling your phone for hours.'

Knowing Karen that probably meant she'd tried once or twice. 'I must have left it in the cottage,' Veronica said, refusing to feel guilty after all the times she had tried to get hold of her sister. 'It's acting a bit erratically at the moment.' She might have been talking about herself, she thought ruefully.

'Probably because she over-cooked her SIM card when she left the phone on the dashboard of the car while we were having lunch yesterday,' said Luc.

Veronica wasn't going to play the blame game. After all, who was responsible for her forgetting it in the first place? Luc had no right to be so distracting.

'Did she give you any message for me?'

'Well, the signal was breaking up a lot by the time I got on the line—Ashley took the call initially, but I'm not sure what they said to each other because she and Ross have gone off to dinner and an arts festival performance in Avignon. From what I could make out, Karen said they're having a tropical storm, which has apparently meant a few changes of scene. They're on some remote island where they were going to do a photographic shoot on a boat, but that's put off for a few days…'

Karen had been highly excited that they were going to spend part of the time aboard a luxury super-yacht owned by some local gazillionaire, Veronica remembered. It seemed that even gazillionaires couldn't control the weather.

'So what does that mean, exactly?' She frowned, not liking what she was hearing.

Melanie's blue eyes took on a look of rueful sympathy that was warning enough for her next words: 'She seemed to think it unlikely she'll get here before you're due to fly home. And now she's in a dilemma because it appears that one of the models knows some fashion maven who has a holiday home in Nassau, and has asked if Karen would like to stay on there for a few extra days after the shoot...'

'Surprise, surprise,' muttered Luc cynically.

Veronica affected not to hear him, although she feared she shared his jaundiced view.

'I see,' she said, her face going hot with embarrassment on behalf of her sister. By the sound of it Karen was dying to snap up the invitation. Given her consistent evasiveness, the possibility of staying on in Nassau had probably been on the cards all along.

From the commiserative expression in Melanie's eyes it was obvious that she suspected the same thing. Knowing what she knew now, Veronica guessed one of the reasons that Karen kept turning up excuses to stay away was probably to avoid being daily confronted with the object of her abortive crush. Her sister might appear to be cheerfully immune to rejection, but only because she had always deleted her mortifying failures from her consciousness and thus had never had to face the consequences of her behaviour—or learn from her mistakes. Until now. Setting her sights on a relative of her employer had been stupid, even for Karen.

However, Veronica was in no position to cast stones. She couldn't really blame Karen for seizing the chance to escape a potentially awkward predicament, given her own panicked reaction to facing Luc again and vain attempts to ignore him!

'For my part, I told her that we're actually managing very well without her now that things have settled down. But of course I said I couldn't speak for you,' Melanie added hurriedly.

'You don't have to tiptoe around, Mel. I've told Veronica about Karen's brief career as my stalker,' interrupted Luc.

Melanie looked pained. 'Hardly a stalker, Luc, she just went through a little phase. We've all made idiots of ourselves at some stage—I remember you had a crush on that dreadful young woman who was your Maths tutor when you were sitting your scholarship exams.'

She looked slightly aghast as soon as the words were out, but Luc merely grinned. 'Anne had an IQ of one hundred and forty.'

Melanie's tension dissolved into a laugh. 'Oh, well—that explains why you kept dropping things for her to pick up whenever she wore those tiny miniskirts and tube tops—it was her IQ you were really drooling over!'

She turned her attention apologetically back to Veronica.

'When we originally made our plans, Luc didn't think he was going to be able to make it for more than a day or two. It was only when he freed up a block of his time that poor Karen began to get a wee bit less enthusiastic about having the cottage while we were here. But, maybe this is fate—I mean, if you *did* manage to change the date of your flight home, you could either stay on here until Karen does turn up, or do as I suggested and go back up to take another bite at Paris. What do you think? Either way we'd adore to have you...'

'I couldn't have worded it better myself,' murmured Luc for Veronica's ears alone.

Her colour deepened, and, mistaking the reason, Melanie added kindly: 'Of course, you might have other ideas. I know you've set an October deadline to get Out Of The Box fully functional, and you've already got someone contracted to deliver the application for your website, so you may be keen to rush back. Just remember, it won't cost you anything extra in terms of accommodation if you do stay. Let me know after you've had a little think about it.

'Anyway, I told Karen you'd call her back...even though

you might not have much luck until the storm passes over. You can use the phone here if yours isn't working. And don't worry about the charges—thanks to my book it's all a write-off to my taxes!'

Needless to say, in spite of her best efforts Veronica was unable to raise her elusive sister, and hanging up the receiver after her final attempt she was about to slip back to the cottage to obsess over all the tantalising possibilities encapsulated in *'hold that thought'* when she ran across Sophie, who wanted to show off her room.

'It's upstairs on the corner. I can see the pool from my window. That's how I knew you were down there today,' she confided. 'I was going to come and swim with you, because I'm not allowed in the pool by myself, but then stupid Ross was there,' she said glumly.

Reminded of her obligation, Veronica allowed herself to be led to the big wooden staircase, past the gutted ground-floor bathroom, where Miles was already back at work, grouting a stretch of blue ceramic tiles in the huge sunken tub.

'No rest for the wicked!' His eyes crinkled over the top of his paper breathing mask as they poked their heads in to view the progress, Sophie wrinkling her nose at the strong chemical smell of adhesive.

Sophie's room was bigger than her one at home, she reported as Veronica admired the high, beamed ceiling and dark, polished wooden floor offset by white walls and a pretty lavender-motif bedspread on the double bed, which matched the curtains on the two windows, one looking out onto the kitchen courtyard, the other the garden and one corner of the pool.

'Gran says that this can be my room every time I come to stay,' said the girl, explaining the origins of the rocks and ornaments she had collected since she had arrived, and arranged in neat rows on the chest of drawers. As Veronica sat on the bed Sophie opened the towering oak wardrobe that stood in the corner and proudly showed off the neat collection of clothes that only took up a small corner of the cavernous interior.

'Be careful you don't fall in and end up in Narnia,' Veronica delighted her by commenting.

'*The Lion, The Witch and The Wardrobe* is one of my favourite stories—I love all the Narnia books!'

Throwing herself onto her stomach on the bed beside Veronica, she gave her an oddly assessing look before seeming to make a decision. She wriggled forward to hang upside down and drag a bulging, square book from under the bed.

'This is the scrapbook about Luc I've been making,' she said shyly, hauling it up onto the bed and opening the patterned cardboard cover. 'I brought it over to show him. See—Mum gave me all the old cuttings she had about him so it starts when he was still at school.' She turned the pages of yellowing newsprint. 'Whenever we see his name in the papers or on the Internet, or he sends me stories about himself from overseas, I paste them in. And I stick in some of his letters and the things he sends me, like programmes and cool autographs and pictures of him with famous people. He was real impressed when he saw it. He said I could be his official biographer,' she said proudly. 'That means I can write the story of his life. I think I might be a writer, like Mum, one day. I'm good at collecting information and I always get A for my essays.'

'Not a builder, like Dad?' murmured Veronica, dying to snatch the treasure-trove and pore over the fascinating contents.

'I don't think I'm going to be big enough,' Sophie said seriously. 'And I'm a bit clumsy at doing fiddly things. Luc says it's because my brain is too busy concentrating on important stuff.'

Veronica's attention was caught by a crumpled loose page sticking out at the back of the book, her heart accelerating as she realised it was from an English equivalent of the French tabloid she had picked up on the train, and featured a very familiar strip of photographs.

'I haven't had time to stick this one in yet,' Sophie said, tugging it free and smoothing it carefully on top of the scrap-book. 'Ashley bought the paper at the airport and it's been stuffed in her luggage, so I'll have to iron it first.'

'That's Max Foster.' Sophie's stubby finger unnecessarily identified the pugnacious Scottish action-film star in the top photo. 'Luc got me his autograph last year. And, see—there's Luc squidged between him and that blonde lady—'

A very beautiful blonde lady, Veronica amended. The first two photographs of the trio at a restaurant table were murky and pixelated, as if snapped by a cell phone in low lighting, others of the two men in a wild scuffle were better lit but blurred by movement—specifically the big fist mashing into Luc's half-obscured face. Wild-eyed Max Foster hogged most of the camera, looking like a dissipated copy of the macho char-acters the forty-five-year-old actor played on the big screen, and notoriously carried over into his turbulent private life.

It was no wonder she hadn't recognised Luc at a glance, Veronica thought as she stared at the dark, grainy pictures. As well as being slightly out of focus in most of the shots, he was dressed with alien black-tie formality, and against his inky jacket his pony-tail was invisible, leaving his hair looking as if it were cropped short.

The accompanying text tagged Luc variously as a 'secre-tive tycoon' and 'mystery millionaire' reputed to be a 'long-time close friend' and 'frequent private companion' to Elise Malcolm, the thirty-eight-year-old wife of a rising star in the House of Commons. Andrew Malcolm's demands for strong moral leadership and emphasis on his own stable home-life, incorruptible principles and squeaky-clean background were rapidly building him a political power-base, and his attrac-tive, Oxford-educated wife was considered one of his vital social assets.

According to the copy, Max Foster had been 'off his face'

when he entered the restaurant of the small and exclusive Mayfair hotel to join Lucien Ryder at his table. But when the 'fuming millionaire' took exception to offensive remarks about Elise Malcolm he followed the actor to the restroom and their 'furious slugfest' had spilled out into the hall, only ending when hotel security staff had pulled the two angry men apart.

There was a great deal of speculative innuendo about the words that had given such offence, and what the 'elusive financier' and his 'distraught companion, nervously fingering her wedding ring' had been doing having a late-night supper in a restaurant that catered solely to hotel residents and their invited guests. Much was made of the fact that, since rumours of the incident had begun swirling nearly a fortnight before the photographs had surfaced in the press, Andrew Malcolm had been conspicuously silent about the state of his ten-year marriage.

Careful to avoid libel by actually stating it, the paper was inviting the inference that Foster's drunken antics had blown the whistle on Luc's long-standing affair with Malcolm's wife.

'Does Luc know you've got this?' Veronica asked carefully, fighting a sudden urge to tear the thing into a million separate pieces. Sophie was too young to read between the lines of the report—to her it was just a story about a fight Luc had with a famous film star.

But Sophie surprised her. 'Of course he does,' she said. 'I already showed him the whole scrapbook. Mum doesn't want me to put this in, but Luc said that would be like censorship—if I'm going to keep a record of his life then it should be a proper one that shows the bad as well as the good. He said a biography isn't true to life if it doesn't show a person warts and all…'

But this was a rather large, ugly and disfiguring wart, Veronica thought unhappily. The kind of painful blemish that could create scandals, wreck careers…and break hearts.

No wonder Luc hadn't wanted her to know about it. She

half wished now that she didn't, but it was too late to turn back the clock.

Just as she was lecturing herself not to jump to damaging conclusions on flimsy evidence from a tainted source the way she had over Karen, she looked up to see Luc in the doorway, and couldn't help her guilty start at his realisation of what she and Sophie were holding.

His smile died, his face turning to carved granite, and to Veronica's despair the shimmering skein of invisible awareness that had vibrated between them ever since Paris suddenly winked out of existence.

CHAPTER EIGHT

ANOTHER flash of sheet lightning and warning grumble of thunder made Veronica jump nervously as she put her hand to the weathered wooden door at the top of the narrow flight of stone steps. The sky had been growing progressively darker since lunch-time, thickening cloud turning the usual azure to a very deep mauve, and now the distant flashing and crashing that had been rolling around for the last half hour was rapidly moving too close for comfort. Back in New Zealand thunderstorms were short and sharp, heralded by driving rain, but although the swirling breeze had picked up a little, it still felt hot and dry against her skin.

She was unprepared when the unlatched door swung open at the pressure of her touch. She peered into the dim interior, her tentative knock on the thick door-post producing only a soundless thud.

'Luc?'

She could see a couch and several chairs arranged around a stone hearth at one end of the room but no sign of any human occupant. She leaned a little further and caught sight of the corner of a large, rumpled bed. She cleared her throat and raised her voice.

'Luc? Are you in there?'

Suddenly the whole world behind her lit up with blinding

brilliance and almost simultaneously an ear-splitting roar of thunder rattled her bones. With a cry she threw herself inside.

'Luc!'

There was still no answer, and, trembling from mingled fright and apprehension, she edged further into the room. He could be in the bathroom, she thought, eyeing the door on the other side of the bed, which was slightly ajar, revealing a sliver of tile and tub. She couldn't hear any sounds from within, but her ears were still ringing from the thunder.

'Luc, are you there?' She raised her voice to a level he couldn't fail to hear, but there was still no response.

He was unlikely to be far away if he had left his outer door open and a couple of uplights on, she reasoned, wincing at another horrendous crash. She saw a few fat spots of rain hit the flagstones but the brief spatter stopped almost as soon as it started. Regardless, she certainly wasn't going to step outside again while the storm remained directly overhead.

She shivered in spite of the heat. She had an excuse for coming here but it was pretty thin, so perhaps she should indulge her curiosity while she had a chance.

She looked around, coming to the conclusion that Luc was organised without being obsessive—unlike her ex-fiancé, who had always insisted on everything being in its rightful place. There were one or two items of clothing and several books casually strewn around but apart from the unmade bed everything else looked tidy. Perhaps he had been taking a siesta, because the standard fan beside the bed was still rotating its whirring face back and forth, stirring up the sultry air above the king-sized mattress. Against the wall beside the wardrobe was a large desk on which his open laptop sat, next to a neat stack of papers and bound documents anchored by Luc's distinctive silver cell phone.

Unfortunately her own still hadn't recovered from its heatstroke, but today she had at long last managed to have a proper conversation with her sister. Now at least they both knew where they stood.

To her surprise Karen had sheepishly confessed to her idiocy over Luc with little prompting, although casting herself more as a dazzled innocent than a seductive man-chaser. Veronica generously forgave her the face-saving explanation, although they both knew that Karen was very far from being an innocent—having been sexually active much earlier than her older sister, often teasing Veronica for her old-fashioned attitudes about love and romance.

As usual, Karen had got her way—she was going to stay in Nassau before linking up with Melanie about where and when to resume her job.

But this time Veronica, too, was getting exactly what she wanted: freedom to make her own choices, unfettered by responsibility for her sister.

If only she could work out what those choices were.

In the frustrating two days since Luc had seen her with Sophie's scrapbook she hadn't had a chance to speak to him alone. Now, whenever they ventured out on some Melanie-inspired jaunt, either Zoe or Sophie were invited along.

Veronica was beginning to get an inkling of what the tabloid press meant when they called him 'elusive'. Even when he was physically present Luc had an infuriating ability to make himself inaccessible—to withdraw into himself while remaining seemingly relaxed and sociable. He had also taken to vanishing into his room for long sessions on his laptop, although Melanie saw nothing unusual in his behaviour.

'Luc claims he's much more laid-back than he used to be, but he can never stay away from work for long,' she had sighed to Veronica when they encountered each other on the regular morning trek to the *boulangerie*. 'He'd be lost without that computer of his—it's practically grafted onto his body.'

'And I wonder where he gets that from!' humphed Zoe from

her daughter's other side. 'You're supposed to be on a break, too, and yet here you are sneaking in all this "research" and look at Miles and that bathroom—talk about a busman's holiday!'

So it was only Veronica who saw anything dramatically different in Luc's manner over the past two days.

He was being polite to her…and she hated it!

She was also bewildered. She understood that Luc might not have wanted to say anything upsetting in front of Sophie, but later she had expected him to be angry or acidly defensive—or at the very least to laugh off that newspaper cutting as the toxic piece of gutter journalism it was, but instead he had arrogantly declined to react at all, leaving Veronica suspended in an emotional limbo.

Veronica picked up the sterling silver pen that lay beside the laptop, noting the engraved initials on the side of the barrel. It must have been a gift, she mused, because, given his love of privacy, she couldn't imagine Luc buying himself anything that advertised his identity, even via a discreet monogram.

The pen was heavy and cool in her hand, the ballpoint already extended for work. She could picture Luc at the desk, his clever face taut with concentration, his strong fingers cradling the monogrammed shaft as he made the spiky, closely written notes on the lined pad next to the computer. In a silly impulse worthy of Karen, she couldn't resist tearing off the top sheet of a small, square memo pad and bending over to write a few experimental words with his expensive pen, enjoying the smooth, sensuous glide of the fine black tip.

'Leaving me a note?' The clipped question was punctuated by another blinding flash out the windows and instant clap of monstrous thunder.

Veronica jerked upright, choking off her scream as she saw Luc kick the outer door closed and dump an armload of clean laundry obviously rescued from the clothes-line on a nearby chair. He was barefoot, wearing pale chinos and a faded grey Oxford University tee shirt spotted with a few drops of rain. When he bent to pick up a fallen shirt Veronica quickly thrust the little square of blue paper into the back pocket of her snug white denim shorts.

'Or perhaps you were searching my room for something else,' he said, heavily sarcastic. 'Some compromising piece of information that might confirm your worst opinions about me? Or something you might be able to hawk to the tabloids—I understand they're offering substantial sums for tell-all stories about me, and you could sell them a whopper, couldn't you?'

His toxic sarcasm was music to her thunderstruck ears. Finally, she had caught him sufficiently off-guard to get past that cool barrier of politeness and the connection between them was suddenly back, full-force, awareness of his seething energy slamming into her with the power of a physical blow.

'No, actually I was looking for you. I called out, but there was no answer—'

His insolent sneer was reflected in the sullen rake of his dark eyes. 'So you came in anyway.'

If that wasn't calling the kettle black! thought Veronica.

'I wanted to get in out of the storm—I've always hated thunderstorms…' She shivered as white light strobed through the gap in the half-drawn shutters. 'I thought you might be in the bathroom. I…I was just trying out your pen,' she said lamely, holding it up. 'It's beautiful.'

'It was a graduation present, given to me when I got my first degree.' He raised his voice over the next roll of thunder as he strolled over to pluck it from her hand.

'Aren't you going to ask who gave it to me?' he challenged with sharp antagonism.

She sensed a trap and decided that there was no avoiding it. She shrugged, her shoulders sliding against the thin silk of her short-sleeved blouse. 'Elise Malcolm?'

His black brows snapped down over his quarrelsome
eyes. 'How the hell could you possibly know that?' he demanded furiously.

She tossed her head, the fiery glints in her hair sparking
defiantly in the artificial glow from the uplights. 'I didn't—
it was just a lucky guess. That newspaper said you'd known
each other a long time.'

He glowered at her mention of the tabloid. 'We were at
Oxford together.'

'Really?' Veronica held his gaze steadily, even though her
heart stuttered at the taut statement. 'Together' had a totally
different connotation from 'at the same time'.

'Well, all I can say is that she obviously has good taste.'

His eyes narrowed and she realised her unintended *double
entendre* had momentarily thrown him. She could see him
silently debating whether she was referring to him or the pen.
His hand clenched around the silver barrel.

'Don't you want to ask *why* she gave it to me?' he ground
out, his voice thick with frustration at her refusal to cooperate.

'You just told me—to celebrate your graduation.' Her
calm acceptance seemed only to inflame his already dangerous temper.

'Because we were sleeping together!' His harsh truth exploded in her ears like another crash of thunder as he threw
the pen onto the desk. 'Elise and I pretended to be just friends
but we were secretly at it like rabbits every chance we got.
Isn't that what you wanted to know?'

Were. The word sank into her consciousness and she clung
to it like a lifeline. He was using the past tense. She allowed
the certainty to saturate her awareness. But she had waited a
moment too long to respond.

'What's the matter? Not shocking enough? Haven't I given
you enough salacious detail?' He swooped like a hawk on her
hesitation, revealing the savagely offended pride that was at

the core of his bitter fury: 'That's why you came snooping around up here, isn't it? You want to know if I'm the adulterous bastard they say I am—'

'No—that's not why I—'

'Well, you're not the only one who can go on a snooping expedition,' he interrupted roughly. 'You have quite a lurid recent past yourself, don't you, Veronica? Let's see what I came up with…' He leaned over the desk to punch a key on his computer and the screen-saver dissolved into an Internet search page. Another couple of clicks and Veronica was mortified to find herself staring at Neil Ordway's web-page, the one that had lately caused her so much hassle and unwelcome attention. On it he was promoting himself as a candidate on the reality TV show *Second Chances* in which people who were rejected in love tried again to win over the partner of their choice, with the help of a 'romantic adviser' and an intrusive camera crew following their every date.

'Well, well, well, there are quite a few news links to this little gem! I see you were engaged last year, but you jilted the poor guy at the altar a few weeks after he had a multimillion-dollar lottery win. What went wrong—did he ask you to sign a pre-nup?' he said sardonically.

Veronica flushed with remembered pain and outrage. 'No, actually, he had wonderful plans for us both to share it. He kept his big win a secret until just before the wedding when he told me he'd bought a dairy farm for us to live on after we were married—contrary to everything we'd planned together,' she said flatly, reliving the horrendous row the night before the wedding, which had exposed the myth that they were a partnership of equals and confirmed that her multiplying doubts about the man she was to marry were more than the usual bridal jitters.

'Well, now he's telling everyone he wants another chance at a new life with you,' he taunted, scrolling down the page.

'No, he doesn't, he just won't admit his own mistakes,' she said, shouldering past him to quit the application before he could read out any more. 'All isn't as rosy as he thought on his farm and he blames me. He's never forgiven me for not turning up at the church, even though I'd told him the night before that the wedding was off. He thinks that he can humiliate me into taking him back—or, failing that, just humiliate me. Fortunately, the TV company is on a strict time schedule, and they can't film his story if I won't cooperate.'

He caught her elbow when she drew back, bitter triumph at her discomfiture lurking in the dark brown eyes. 'Not very nice, is it, Veronica, to have people publicly pawing over the intimate details of your private life, and hounding you for comments—?'

'No, it's horrible—but then I don't have the luxury of all the firewalls that you can afford to throw up around you—'

'Damn it, you don't think I feel just as exposed?' he demanded ferociously. 'Constantly having to defend myself to people like you, who try, judge, and condemn me out of hand—'

'How can I know what your feelings are if you don't talk about them? And I never *condemned* you—'

He gave a raw laugh. 'I saw the way you cringed from me when I came into Sophie's room.'

Was *that* what he'd thought?

'That was because I felt guilty, that's all!' she cried. 'You make me feel as if being curious about you is some kind of crime—'

'Curiosity? Is that what it is?' He caught her other arm as she tried to shake him loose. 'Exactly what kind of curiosity are we talking about? Why don't you tell me what it is about me that you find most fascinating?' he invited savagely.

Lightning flashed and Veronica instinctively squeezed her

eyes shut and tensed, waiting for the thunder, but this time it was a couple of seconds before it raged off in the near distance.

She gingerly opened her eyes and found his combative expression tempered by faintly cruel amusement. 'You really are twitchy about storms, aren't you?' he scorned.

'I saw a cow killed by a lightning strike in a paddock when I was a child.' Her hands unconsciously gripped his restraining forearms, reassuring herself they were both safe. 'I've been a bit storm-shy ever since.'

His amusement faded. 'That was probably fork lightning. This is sheet lightning—discharging up in the air, within the cloud itself—only dangerous if you're a bird or a plane. It's true,' he added as she looked at him, her grey eyes deeply dubious. 'I'm a certified genius—I know all sorts of useful facts.' His mouth took on an ironic twist. 'Would I lie to you?'

There was another flash and instant crack and she jumped, instinctively moving closer to his sheltering chest. 'Oh, I was sure it was moving away!'

'I used to come and holiday here with Zoe sometimes during my university breaks. When there's been a big build-up of static in the clouds, these dry summer storms can crash and bash back and forth across the plateau for ages,' he said, subtly easing them further away from the window by the desk. 'Once, when I was staying here as a kid with Zoe and Fred I timed a continuous storm at two hours—although technically, I suppose, it was actually a series of storm cells.'

Veronica's eyes rounded in dismay and he uttered an arid laugh. 'Afraid you might be trapped with me until it passes?'

A tiny frisson passed through her body and his gaze sharpened into a keen alertness that drove her rashly into speech.

'I'm not a coward...unlike someone else I could name,' she said with a haughty disdain that instantly made him hard. 'You accuse *me* of making unfounded assumptions but you're the one putting words in my mouth and then refusing to listen—'

'I'd rather put something else in your mouth,' he muttered, shocking her out of her flimsy sandals.

A flush joined up all the freckles on her face, and she went hot all over. 'Is sex all you ever think about?'

'What made you think I was talking about sex?' he shot back innocently. 'Maybe I was going to offer you a drink.'

He watched as she went an even more intriguing shade of red, remembering the rosy flush that had mantled her whole body when she had orgasmed astride him in Paris. She hadn't been so haughty with him then! She had been all heat and trembling passion, delectably eager to try things that were obviously new to her. Her fiancé must have been a real dunce in bed, he thought smugly, his eyelids drooping as he contemplated an entirely new curriculum for his passionate protégé.

'You're trying to distract me from my point—'

'Am I succeeding?' he said dreamily, from the depths of his orgasmic trance.

She was unnerved by his intense, heavy-lidded expression of slumberous speculation, and her thoughts tangled into confusion.

'Yes—I mean, no!'

Where had all his former anger gone? It appeared to have dissolved into something infinitely more disturbing. The air in the room was suddenly thick to breathe, hot and humid in her labouring lungs.

'Pity.' He lifted a hand to gently tuck a stray strand of her hair behind her burning ear, blowing a gentle breath over the dew of perspiration that had sprung out on her smooth, lightly freckled brow. 'You look as if you can do with something long and tall to cool you off,' he murmured huskily.

Her eyes involuntarily flicked down over his length and he laughed, this time with genuine, deep-throated humour. 'Oh, yes, I can see you really are an ideas girl, aren't you?'

'I don't know what you're talking about—'

'Liar,' he chided her lazily. 'The trouble with me is that

I'm not in the least bit cool where you're concerned…I'm very, very hot…'

'That's not the way you've been acting for the last couple of days,' she said doggedly.

'I can prove it.' He suddenly let her go and pulled the faded tee shirt over his head, throwing it carelessly onto the floor. 'Feel me,' he said, grasping her wrists and placing her hands flat on his naked chest, uttering a teasing hiss as her palms made contact. 'See how I sizzle for you.'

'What do you think you're doing?' she croaked, aware of his flat nipples peaking in the hollow of her hands. She hadn't realised that happened to men, too…

'What I should have done days ago,' he admitted, gathering her loosely up in his arms, aroused by the fact that in spite of her sulky protests she didn't struggle. 'Then we wouldn't have had this little misunderstanding…'

Little!

'And whose fault is that?' she accused as they stood nose to nose, the slight heel on her sandal banishing the difference in their heights.

There was a white flicker at the edge of her vision, but she forgot to count the gap to the thunder as he sank his teeth gently into the lush pout of her lower lip.

'Mine, all mine,' he said soothingly, flicking at the bite with his tongue and sucking on it gently as he stroked his hands up and down her silk-covered back, moulding her to his lean form, enjoying the feel of her lace-encased breasts begging for attention through the thin fabric of her blouse.

'Too much thinking and not enough action. But I promise I'll make it up to you,' he said, turning his pledge into a lavish kiss that explored every cleft and crevice of her mouth. Before she could catch her breath, his hand moved up between their bodies to slip free the buttons of her blouse. In almost the same movement he released the front catch of her bra, hidden beneath a pretty bow. To the applause of thunder and lightning he stripped both garments back off her shoulders, growling with carnal hunger as they melded skin to skin. She slid her arms around his neck to increase the delicious friction of her breasts against his chest as they swayed in an increasingly heated exchange of kisses, fumbling with their remaining clothes.

Luc pushed a finger into the upturned cuff of her shorts at the side-seam, and ran it teasingly around to the seam at her inner thigh.

'Did I tell you how sexy I think you look in these?' he murmured as his finger traced up to toy with her zip. 'I love the way they hug your delicious peach of a bottom, but I think you look even sexier out of them....'

She trembled when she felt the rasp of his hair-roughened legs against her smooth thighs, the straining hardness of his body as he ripped aside the tumbled bedclothes and pushed her down beneath him on the bed, pausing only long enough to grab a small packet from the leather kit bedside table and don protection with the same patient finesse that he had shown in Paris.

But there was little finesse in the way he fell on her.

'God, I'm sorry—' His eyes were glittering hectically, his face deeply flushed as he pushed her thighs apart so that he could surge between them, testing her humid heat with his blunt shaft, fighting to control the overwhelming urge to seek his own satisfaction at the expense of her pleasure. His biceps bulged as he braced himself above her, trying to protect her from his rampant eagerness. 'Don't!' he rasped warningly as her hand sought to cup and caress his heavy masculinity, her thumb teasing at the sensitive tip through the thin sheath, but it was too late and with a hoarse cry he thrust through the delicate cradle of her fingers and buried himself to the hilt in her welcoming tightness.

He looked down at her with eyes full of agonised surprise,

her supple fingers trapped between them only adding to his perilous excitement. 'It wasn't supposed to happen this fast,' he gritted.

Aglow with a wonderful sexual confidence that only Luc had ever made her feel, she laughed deep in her belly, feeling herself vibrate around him, and lifted her head to nip at his sweaty chest, loving him for caring enough to want to wait for her to join him in ecstasy. But she didn't want him in control, she wanted him wild and reckless, the elemental Luc, holding nothing back...

'And here I was wondering why you were being such a slowcoach,' she teased in her distinctive deep voice, squirming and tilting her hips so that she could take him deeper, twining her long legs around his waist to seal herself intimately against him and throwing her arms over her head so that her breasts lifted provocatively towards his mouth.

He uttered a low, guttural sound, and, while thunder and lightning played outside, Veronica exultantly embraced a whirlwind tempest of her own, pierced with violent delight as Luc stormed his way into her body, her heart, her soul... hoarsely shouting out her name in wrenching pleasure as he shuddered to his extravagant completion.

She was even more charmed by Luc's evident chagrin when he withdrew and rolled pantingly onto his side, looked slightly dazed by the experience.

'Are you *blushing*?' she teased as he stripped off the used protection. 'Don't worry, I promise I won't tell anyone about your lack of stamina,' she added, basking in playful amusement at his expense, knowing that his bred-to-the-bone masculinity was equal to the challenge.

His eyes smouldered above his dark-smudged cheekbones as he looked at her lolling voluptuously against his mounded pillows, her bare breasts quivering as she tried to repress her giggles.

'Think that was funny, do you?' he drawled, a dangerous smile stealing across his mouth.

He jackknifed out of the bed and padded without embarrassment into the bathroom, flaunting the gorgeous, tight backside that had been a feature of her recent fantasies, and then over to the small refrigerator hidden in a wooden cabinet, coming back with a rattling jug of ice cubes, which he set down on the bedside table.

'I've been looking forward to this,' he purred, scooping the first ice cube out of the jug and prowling back onto the bed, blatantly displaying to Veronica's fascinated gaze that he was already semi-aroused, even though it had only been a few minutes since his shattering release. 'Let's see who has the last laugh now…'

Her laughter soon turned to squeals as the frozen cube stuck to her skin with an exciting burn, but it almost immediately began to melt and Luc began to trace intricate patterns all over her body, paying special attention to the most sensitive nooks and crannies, chasing the ice slivers with his tongue as they dissolved on her silky-hot skin.

In spite of the diminishing jug of ice cubes her body was soon suffused with heated tension and Luc leaned over and flicked a switch on the fan to stop it rotating, directing the smooth flow of air across her slick body, adding a piquant wind-chill factor to the effects of his wickedly applied ice. He teased arctic circles around and over her nipples, moulding them into frigid stiffness, following the ice-burning chill with the scalding heat of his mouth as he suckled to a thaw the frosty peaks. Then he shocked her by drawing the dripping ice cube down over her quivering belly and through the soft thicket on her womanly mound until it slipped into the crease between her legs. She gasped at the glacial caress, but he quelled her brief struggle with seductive promises, drawing the cube again and again along the secret folds, teasing her until she begged again for the exquisite heat of his mouth.

He coaxed the last ice cube into her mouth, kissing her as she clattered it around against her teeth and let the icy droplets trickle down her throat. When the sensitive inside of her mouth was almost numb with cold he whispered a wicked invitation in her ear and she quivered as she grazed her icy lips down the centre of his body, at the mercy of his cleverly caressing hands as she made him groan by pushing her frigid tongue into his shallow navel, and then shudder and moan when she reached her goal and froze him with her deep, loving kiss. His hands plunged into her thick, tangled locks as his back arched and his hips surged, his thighs cording as the tension ripped through his muscles.

'Oh, no, not this time,' he growled, drawing her up beside him, and pinning her spread-eagled to the bed. 'You say I don't tell you how I feel. Let me show you…'

The final, sexy flourish was when he rose above her on his knees and—just as he had in Paris—reached up to release his hair from its confinement, shaking his head, so that his glossy black mane skimmed across the top of his muscular shoulders, sliding forward to flare in a veil around their faces as he kissed her and rocked her with him to sweet oblivion.

Afterwards, as she drowsed exhausted in his arms, he was the one who wanted to talk.

'So, tell me about this creepy ex-fiancé of yours…'

She was too relaxed to hold anything back as she told him about her abortive wedding. Neil had thought his windfall would solve all their problems, but it had only exacerbated them. It had been a huge shock to Veronica that he would make such a momentous decision about their future lives together without even consulting her…especially when the farm he had chosen was in a particularly isolated area where there was no phone line, let alone access to the Internet. He had known that she had no interest in farming and had only stayed on in the country out of obligation to her parents. He had always lived in a large town and boasted that rural banking was merely his stepping-stone to a city bank job. He had claimed to understand her desire to live an urban lifestyle— to travel and run a business, and to bring up her children where there was a choice of schools. And yet Neil had assumed that when he presented her with a *fait accompli* she would meekly bow to his superior judgement.

'Jerk!' Luc sneered. 'But you must have loved him once,' he said, arranging a swathe of her hair across the pillow.

'I thought you decided I was marrying him for his money!' she said, and sighed when he didn't respond to the provocative evasion. 'Partly, I think, it was because I was so eager to get out in the wider world and experience life. Neil and I seemed to share the same aspirations—or so I thought. I loved who I *thought* he was—only he turned out to be someone completely different, someone I didn't even *like*—'

'Not to mention a total loony,' said Luc, sounding annoyingly smug.

'I have terrible taste in men,' she agreed, but he merely smiled.

'Until now,' he pointed out.

Since it was too hot to remain entwined for long, he propped his head on his hand as he lay on his side, his dark hair winnowing slightly in the breeze from the fan.

He lazily told her something of his childhood with his father, a dare-devil character who was a great natural teacher and fiercely determined to be a good father to his only son, always encouraging him to watch, listen and learn, to question and inquire. When he touched on the difficulties of being intellectually advanced for his age, and his move to Oxford, Veronica suddenly wasn't so drowsy any more. She hardly dared breathe for fear of spooking him, but then he casually mentioned the unmentionable:

'I met Elise when I was sixteen—she was doing a post-grad when I was in my first year. She was my tutor for a while and I fell boyishly in love amongst the "dreaming spires".'

'Sixteen!' She sat up, unable to help her burst of fierce outrage. 'Why, that's practically cradle-robbing! She's nearly ten years older than you. What does a twenty-five-year-old woman want with a sixteen-year-old boy?' She scowled.

He grinned at her charming naivety. 'I was a very mature sixteen-year-old,' he said modestly. 'But, rest easy, love, I only lusted from afar. She was beautiful, witty, and sophisticated and much preferred men to boys. I didn't get to actually sleep with her until I was eighteen and fully grown. Even then I was a borderline case as far as she was concerned, which was why we kept it quiet. Which was lucky because she'd fallen in with the political set and decided she wanted to marry Andrew.' He sounded more cynical than enamoured, she thought in relief.

'And this matters to me—why?' she said loftily, clasping her arms around her updrawn legs. It didn't mean anything that he called her 'love', she lectured herself sternly. He probably just used it as a generic term.

'Well, since you did come slinking in to ferret out my secrets…' he said, stroking a finger up and down her bare hip.

'Actually, I didn't,' she sniffed, trying to ignore the suggestive stirring in his loins. 'I came looking for you because Melanie said Justin was coming up from Marseilles on the train tomorrow and since you needed to do a few things in Avignon she'd asked you to pick him up from the station. She suggested I go with you and have a look around the old city. I was going to ask if that would be all right—'

'And that's *all* you wanted me for?'

'Yes!' she lied brashly, without batting an eyelash.

He tilted his head, so that his hair slithered sexily against his cheek, catching on the dark fuzz of his jaw, giving her a bone-melting look of regret. 'So I guess there's no point in asking you to make love again?

She launched herself at him in a laughing flurry of rounded limbs.

'Only if this time I get to use the ice cubes!'

CHAPTER NINE

'*CIAO*.' Justin acknowledged Veronica's greeting with an engaging grin as he and Luc walked out of the Avignon Centre train station and across the road to the Porte de la République entrance to the walled city, where she had found a convenient patch of shade in which to shelter from the mid-afternoon sun.

'I'd say it was cool to see you, but I think "Phew, what a scorcher!" would be more appropriate.' Justin's teeth flashed white against his tan as he switched his bulging backpack to his other shoulder. He was several inches shorter than Luc, his light brown hair streaked by the sun, his manicured stubble and casually trendy clothes making a definite style statement. 'It was pretty sweltering in Rome and not much better in Marseilles, but at least the friend who put me up there had air-con, and we could dunk ourselves in the Med with the girls in the string bikinis whenever we began to brown around the edges.'

He was as mischievous as she remembered from their previous brief encounters. 'You're looking very Italian,' she remarked with a smile.

He laughed and saluted her with a lift of his sunglasses, revealing bright blue eyes. '*Grazie, signorina!* In an Italian hotel kitchen you either assimilate or die.' He glanced over her bright sundress, noting the accessorised drink bottle and camera, and give-away comfortable walking sandals. 'And you're looking very French Tourist Chic. Especially the hat. Bargain at the market, was it?'

'Yes, it was,' she admitted, amused by his cheek.

Passing through the towering, medieval stone walls, they turned into the bustling, tree-lined street running up towards the square where Veronica and Luc had had coffee before he had patiently followed her fascinated meanderings through the nearby Palace of the Popes. They had arrived in Avignon early, so that Luc could show her the highlights of the historic city before the heat and crowds flocking to festival events began to clog the streets, and Veronica's head was filled with intoxicating sights, sounds and experiences.

And not only her head, she thought, with a sideways glance at Luc, looking relaxed and sinfully sexy in his jeans and dark red shirt. Her heart fluttered in her breast. You'd never know from his air of crisp vitality and fluid, loose-limbed stride that he'd spent a mostly sleepless night of energetic activity.

As she had herself. Veronica adjusted the brim of her hat to screen her glowing cheeks from her companions. Every now and then she found herself bathed in honey-coated memories of their secret tryst. The afternoon in Luc's bed had drifted on into evening and then later that night, after she had refused to join him at the Reeds' dinner table—afraid that she would be unable to hide her tumultuous feelings—he had come to her at the cottage, appearing like a seductive wraith out of the darkness, a bottle of champagne tucked under his arm.

'I didn't want to spend the night without you,' he said simply as he offered her the champagne. 'To celebrate our *second* first night together—'

This time he had made her cry, as well as laugh, with the fierce intensity of his passion, extorting the maximum pleasure from her trembling fulfilment, drinking in her sobs of need even as he sweetly satisfied them, kissing away her tears of exquisite release, not leaving her wide, single bed until dawn crept through the shutters and the village bells tolled to the fading stars.

'How's Ash?' she heard Justin say to Luc in the process of catching up on family news.

'Well, she and Ross had a tiff yesterday and aren't talking—'

'From what she tells me in her emails, they spend half of their lives not talking,' interrupted Justin. 'God, I hope she changes her mind about marrying him. Mum's warned me we all have to be polite, but he's so incredibly up himself!'

They stopped at the corner of the short road to the hotel where Luc had parked the car, and where he and Veronica had returned for a superb lunch at the Michelin-starred restaurant.

'Justin says he's famished, and would like to drop in on an Italian friend who's working here before we leave, so since we've already eaten I've suggested that we meet him back here in a couple of hours,' explained Luc, and Veronica agreed, remembering that he had yet to attend to his own reasons for wanting to come to Avignon. 'We also still have to get a photograph of you dancing "*sur le pont d'Avignon*,"' he teased, ignoring her protests that she could do that when she returned for her overnight stay, before she caught the TGV back to London for her flight home.

Justin handed over his backpack for Luc to lock in the boot of his car and strode jauntily off while Veronica idled up the main street, window-shopping as she waited for Luc to return from stowing the bag. When he rejoined her, Veronica was staring in shock at a very familiar face on a huge poster at a kiosk outside the city's main Tourist Office.

'Did you know he was here?' she blurted when she realised Luc was staring broodingly over her shoulder at Max Foster's dramatic image advertising his appearance in an avant-garde adaptation of Shakespeare.

He shrugged. 'I've heard he comes down every year for

the Avignon Festival—I believe he has a holiday place in Saint Rémy…'

'You don't know? I thought you two were friends—' she said, faltering as she recalled the dubious source of her information.

His face tightened. 'More of an acquaintance. He stayed at my country place a couple of times when he was filming in Derbyshire on one of the films I backed, but not while I was there. He's talented, but he's also arrogant and self-indulgent—which makes for a dangerous drunk.' He was absently rubbing his hawkish nose as he spoke, making Veronica wonder if the tiny kink that marred its perfection had always been there, or was a recent souvenir of a certain famous fist.

His mouth had thinned, and, sensing his darkening mood, Veronica rummaged in her bag and produced her pen. 'Would you like to improve him with a mangy moustache and a few suppurating boils?'

He sucked in a sharp breath of startled laughter. 'I think a set of horns might be more appropriate! Or maybe he's not the one who should be wearing the horns,' he muttered cryptically, turning to look at her as she dropped the pen back in her bag. 'Most women find him wildly attractive?' he challenged.

She kept her eyes flatteringly intent on his face as she wrinkled her brow as if trying to remember the insignificant subject under discussion.

'Who?'

He laughed again, a full-throated, exuberant sound that attracted the smiling attention of passers-by. 'You're so good for my ego!' Still chuckling, he scooped up her hand in his and tugged her along at his side. 'Come on, we have better things to do than hang around here like a pair of damned groupies!'

A little further up the street he stopped her outside a very stylish jewellery store, the kind that had a security guard manning the heavy glass door. 'I shan't be a moment,' he promised as he slipped inside.

She watched through the glass, and when he drew a small object out of his wallet to show the assistant she put a hand to her throat, suddenly realising what he was asking. She was a trifle embarrassed, knowing that although the sterling silver chain and jade pendant had been difficult for her parents to afford at the time, it couldn't possibly compete with the kind of expensive jewellery discreetly displayed in the light-boxes dotted around the store.

However the elegant assistant didn't reel back in disdain at Luc's request, probably because he was leaning casually on the glass counter, totally at ease in the luxurious surroundings, a picture of dark, masculine charm.

As the assistant disappeared into the back room, Luc glanced up and Veronica ducked across to pretend to be admiring the window display, a dazzling array of diamond rings.

Luc grinned at her through the glass shelves, then he straightened, a faint frown drifting across his face. He stiffened, and strode towards the door and out onto the street.

'What's the matter?' asked Veronica as he slid his arm around her, keeping their backs to the street and looking furtively over his shoulder. She tried to follow his gaze but he blocked her movement with his body.

'Keep looking in the window. I don't think he's quite sure, yet, but…if that's who I *think* it is—' He swore virulently as he did another quick sweep of the pavement across the street.

'Which ring do you like? I like that one?' he said, pointing haphazardly into the window. His arm tightened around her waist, pinning her to his side and he nuzzled her neck, using the shade of her brim to disguise the fact he was keeping a wary eye behind them.

'What are you doing?' Unnerved by his behaviour, Veronica twisted in his grasp in time to see a plump little man in a backwards baseball cap and beige cotton waistcoat and trousers festooned with bulging zip pockets start to dodge his way across the busy street, a long-lens camera bumping against his chest, sweat running in rivulets down the sides of his face.

'Hey—yo! Ryder!'

With another curse, Luc hustled Veronica inside the store, directing a burst of French at the security guard who hastily locked the door behind them.

'Who *is* that?' said Veronica as the man vainly gesticulated to the guard to let him in, then mashed himself against the glass to peer in at them, wiping at the haze of perspiration that was fogging up his view.

'No one you want to know. Bloody paparazzi! I should have realised they'd be buzzing round here with the festival on…it's always a drawcard for celebrities and see-me wannabes…'

'I'm not going away until you give me a money-shot, you know, Ryder!' the photographer was yelling through the toughened glass in a cockney accent. 'So you may as well give it up now, and I'll go away and leave you in peace. Remember me from London? I know where you live—!'

'Blackmailing bastard!' ground out Luc as the man banged on the door with the flat of his hand.

'Come on, Ryder—just one exclusive and I'm outta here! Have you seen Foster since he came out of rehab? Are you down here to see his show? Seen Mrs Malcolm lately? She's supposed to be at a health spa but no one can find her—' The man had swapped his heavy, long-lens camera for a smaller, digital SLR, snapping off pictures as fast as his questions. 'You looking at buying your lady some jewellery? Is she anyone we know? Yo! Darlin''—how about taking off the hat, and giving me a nice, big smile—'

'For goodness' sake!' spluttered Veronica as Luc pushed her over towards the counter, out of sight of the door, but the photographer just moved over to the display window and began shooting between the shelves.

'Damn! He's not going to go away. They're like bloody pitbulls when they lock onto a target,' said Luc furiously. 'They staked out my flat in London, but thank God they didn't know about the one in Paris—'

'Perhaps the guard can do something?' suggested Veronica, realising the intrusive attention she had suffered in New Zealand was mild in comparison.

'And make even more of a scene? He'd love that! It's part of the pap technique—goading people into doing something that makes a more dramatic picture. And we don't want to risk bringing down the rest of the pack—where there's one, there's bound to be others…'

'Hey—these are some pretty fancy rings you two were looking at here in the window, Ryder!' The baying hound's words were greatly muffled by the layers of glass, but still audible in the quiet atmosphere of the shop. 'You gonna to buy her one? What's the big occasion?'

'Honestly! He's not very good at goading, if that's the best he can do,' scorned Veronica, firmly suppressing a leap of forbidden yearning.

Luc looked at her with an arrested expression, his eyes travelling down to the cabinet in front of them, holding a small arrangement of very expensive rings, and then back up to Veronica's flushed face, innocent of make-up, her soft eyes bright with indignation and dark with embarrassed empathy.

She could almost see his brain working like lightning behind his suddenly abstracted gaze; dangerous, forked lightning—the kind that raised the hair on the back of your neck, then sizzled you on the spot before you even had time to run, or even recognise you were in peril. Unfortunately, she seemed to have fallen in love with this particular natural hazard, and flight was no longer a desirable option.

'Well, we *could* try giving him what he wants…' he said slowly, his eyes coming back into focus and filling with a strange, liquid warmth that made something inside her quiver.

He reached up and pulled off her hat, dropping it beside them on the counter as she automatically winnowed her fingers through her flattened hair. 'And save both you and I a load of hassles in the process…'

'But—there's no reason for him to be interested in *me*—' Glancing out the window, she could see the photographer's camera had drooped with disappointment as he registered that her hat hadn't been hiding a recognisable face or glamorous beauty.

'Nor me, *per se*. I'm only a target right now because of Elise and now he's seen you with me that makes *you* a potential target, too,' he told her, turning her to face him and running his finger under the strap of her sundress, gently aligning it more precisely over the faint tan-line on her smooth shoulder. 'If you become tabloid fodder here, because of me, it could follow you home, because you can be sure the Kiwi papers would probably pick it up, and what they don't know about us, they'll make up. It might even get your loony ex a fresh batch of publicity for his crass stunts.' As she opened her mouth to protest he gently sealed her lips with the press of his forefinger. 'I know. It's not fair—that's just the way it is. But we could get him off our backs and kill two birds with one stone…'

'What do you mean?' she said warily, her spine tingling at the silky smile that was stealing over his face.

To her shock he cupped her chin and kissed her square on her puzzled mouth, in full view of the snapping camera. 'I mean, that if we can convince him we're engaged, then our scandal value plummets…we're a humdrum social paragraph rather than a titillating piece of spice. We can make our relationship appear to be so cosily domesticated and respectable that no tabloid worth its salt would bother to give us houseroom,' he said, punctuating his words with kisses.

With his mouth on hers, Veronica had never felt less respectable in her life! She was sure there was something fundamentally wrong with his argument, but right now her mind was too clouded to pinpoint the fault.

The assistant, who had came back to show off the new silver clasp that the jeweller had expertly substituted for the broken catch, was taken aback at the activity outside the window, but as Luc fastened the repaired pendant around Veronica's neck he said something that made her light up like a Christmas tree.

'*Anneaux d'enclenchement? Ah, oui!*' She beamed at them both.

As Luc continued to talk Veronica found her right hand grasped and her ring finger meticulously measured.

'What on earth are you telling her?' Veronica whispered, as the young woman began pulling out selected ring boxes and lining them up along the counter.

A translation was no longer required.

'I told you—I'm saving us from the clutches of notoriety,' said Luc. 'How about this one, *chérie*?' he purred, holding up an obscenely large solitaire.

'You must be crazy,' she squeaked, pushing away the garish offering.

'You're right, far too ostentatious,' he drawled, selecting another box. 'We're aiming for boring respectability, not outrageous bling. We better stay away from the pink diamonds, then. How about this heart-shaped one, then—conservative, conventional even…'

He took wicked delight at her confusion as he rapidly plied her with alternatives. Catching sight of the price on one of the boxes, Veronica thought it would serve him right if she took him seriously—she could trade it in for a small car when she got home!

'Ah, yes, now this one looks *much* more like your style…'

She was certain that he was still mocking, and Veronica's

coruscating reply stuck in her throat as she stared at the ring he had removed from its box. It was utterly gorgeous in its severe simplicity—three flawless, round stones set in yellow gold, their brilliance and purity burning with a winter-white fire that flared through the entire spectrum as he tilted the polished facets to the overhead light.

'Look, it could have been custom-made for you,' he murmured, taking ruthless advantage of her semi-hypnotised awe to slide it onto her finger, saluting her acceptance of his devilish temptation with a teasing kiss.

Veronica didn't even hear the little crow as the man outside got his money shot, or notice the attention he had drawn from a knot of curious passers-by.

'It *is* rather beautiful,' she conceded reluctantly, while at the same time giving in to the sinful desire to admire the way it flashed on her hand, delicate in design yet bold in its fiery message, timelessly elegant and enduring, a symbol of perfect love. She flexed her fingers, wallowing in a shameless moment of possessive craving. It was all only a fantasy, after all…

'It's perfect!' he pronounced, giving the assistant a discreet nod over her down-bent head.

Ten minutes later they were slipping out the fortified back entrance to the store, Veronica still in a pale state of trembling shock.

'I thought you just wanted to *pretend*—you didn't have to actually go as far as *buying* it,' she said in a shaken voice, cradling her hand in a protective fist. 'Do you know how much it *cost*?'

'Of course I do. I have the credit-card receipt to prove it,' he pointed out in amusement, his total lack of concern demonstrating that the rich did indeed live in a different country, she thought. 'And I couldn't very well hand it back with that slime-ball still lurking about—that would have wrecked the whole plan!'

'It wasn't a very well thought-out plan, then,' she said starkly. 'I certainly can't keep wearing it around.' She halted while they were still in the deserted lane and tugged off the ring—which she found extraordinarily difficult to remove, considering how easily it had slipped on—and held it out to him. 'I'd be terrified of losing it, or having it stolen before you got a chance to take it back. Besides, you'll need to be able to say it's never been worn, or they might not give you a full refund,' she added, with a little frown at the thought.

His eyes glittered beneath his lowered lids, his mouth quirking, but he took the ring without argument and carefully placed it back in its leather box inside the black velvet jeweller's bag. 'Come on, we'd better make tracks before our getaway is rumbled and we get chased for words to go with the pictures.' When he casually slid the velvet bag into the pocket of his jeans, she was horrified.

'What if there are pick-pockets about? It could be gone before you know it—'

'You really are a worry-wart,' he said, setting off through a series of narrow streets that would take them to the famous St Bénézet bridge while keeping them away from the main thoroughfares. 'Perhaps it *would* be safer if you kept it on,' he suggested. 'After all, jewellery is *de rigueur* here so no one would look twice at it on your hand. And if we do run back into trouble our engagement would seem more authentic if you were still flashing it—'

'No, thank you!' Veronica hurried to cut him off before he could persuade her against her better judgement. She knew it would be extremely unwise for her emotional health to allow herself to wear his ring, even as a temporary minder.

In fact, she brooded, he was actually being quite foolish in assuming that she would simply play along with his decep-tion without extracting some sort of price. Did the man have no sense of self-preservation? she thought crossly. How did he know she wouldn't take the ring from him and refuse to give it back? She could justifiably claim that he had freely given it to her, and she had witnesses—and photographs—to prove it! If she was a real gold-digger, she could even say he asked her to marry him and sue him for breach of promise.

'*Ma petite amie*' she had heard him refer to her at the jeweller's, but he had publicly demonstrated he had more permanent plans for his intimate friend when he had asked to see '*anneaux d'enclenchement*' and placed that ring on a finger traditionally reserved for engagement rings. In fact, he was leaving himself wide-open to extortion if Veronica suddenly decided to insist that she considered herself well-and-truly 'enclenched'.

She was still fretting about the ring several days later as everyone in Mas de Bonnard geared up for Zoe's birthday celebration. Luc hadn't been back to Avignon and she knew there was no safe in the house.

'Well, I hope you've at least got interim insurance on it,' she muttered as she smoothed her short, tropical-print dress down over her hips. She had intended to go over to the house early to offer to help with the preparations for the lavish lunch Melanie was organising, but then Luc had wandered in and, as usual, had thrown her careful plans into disarray.

He showed no sign of cooling off from their sizzling affair, she thought with a profound thrill of delight, blushing as she saw his lazy-eyed survey of approval reflected in the mirror. In fact, he seemed daily more insatiable, no longer waiting until night to inveigle her into his bed—or prowl over to tumble into hers—and increasingly less careful to guard his simmering looks in the company of others. However, Veronica stood firmly on the side of discretion, not only for the sake of protecting her pride and too-vulnerable heart, but because she didn't want to add to the awkward cross-currents in the household as Ashley and Ross's uneven relationship was further strained by Justin's disruptive presence, his coolness towards Ross and natural affinity with his twin leading her fiancé to feel on the outer.

To Veronica, the secrecy surrounding her liaison with Luc only served to intensify the acute sense of intimacy when they were together. All too aware that her holiday was drawing to a close, she was as eager as Luc to make the most of their time together, to store up the precious memories of passion that might help mitigate the pain of eventual loss. But the present joy was worth the future pain, she told herself as each day she fell a little more in love with him, and each night she gave him another piece of her heart along with the generous gift of her passion.

Yesterday he had coolly offered her a first-class ticket from Paris to Auckland, giving her the option to cancel her train to London and flight from Heathrow without having to worry about the financial penalties, but Veronica still hadn't been able to bring herself to make the decision to travel with him to Paris; to face the ending of their affair—there, where it all began...

'Don't look so desolate, *chérie*.' Luc slid his long limbs out of her bed and back into his clothes, raking his blue-black hair from his face. 'You're not responsible for my decisions, or the personal risks I choose to take. There are some losses insurance never covers. I make my own choices, and I won't go bankrupt if the worst happens...'

The worst already had happened—unrequited love was a form of emotional bankruptcy, she thought later as they toasted Zoe's health after she had opened her huge pile of presents, protesting she couldn't possibly afford the excess baggage to take everything home. But many of the gifts from local friends were furnishings and housewares for her new St Romain home, and there were tears in her eyes as she handed out the hugs and thanks.

Justin, slightly merry on the amount of wine-tasting he had

been doing in the company of a local vintner and his wife, chose an unfortunate lull in the conversation as the cake was being cut to say teasingly to Luc:

'Don't we have something else to celebrate, Luc? When are you two lovebirds planning to make your announcement?'

Veronica, standing just behind Luc, blanched as Justin's words rang out in the silence with the clarity of the village bells.

'Young idiot,' growled Luc, steadying his stepbrother's slightly swaying body with an overly firm hand.

'What announcement? What's he talking about?' Melanie's blonde head swivelled towards Luc from where she was overseeing the cutting of the cake, a look of dawning dismay in her blue eyes as she saw his annoyance.

'Oops,' Justin hiccupped and covered his remorseful mouth with his hand. 'Didn't mean to let the cat out of the bag. It's just that I saw you in the jeweller's in Avignon when that photographer was going totally ape outside.' He gave Veronica a woebegone look over Luc's shoulder. 'Sorry, I knew you must have some reason for keeping quiet—thought maybe you didn't want your engagement to take any of the spotlight off Gran on her big day.'

'Well, you've certainly managed to do that,' said Luc drily, although Veronica noticed in the midst of her embarrassment that Zoe was the only family member not looking at him in consternation.

'You never said anything! You could have at least told *me*,' Ashley was berating her twin, while Ross smirked at the idea of someone other than himself on the receiving end of her ire.

'*Your engagement!* Oh, no, Luc, what's going on? What have you done?' Melanie looked almost distraught, thought Veronica uneasily, as Miles placed a protective hand on her uninjured arm.

She stepped forward to explain that it was all a ploy to

throw off an ambush by the paparazzi, but was speared by a savagely restraining look from Luc.

'Really, Mum, it's not what you think—' he said, and Melanie gasped and bit her lip, her eyes softening.

'Luc?' Suddenly another, soft, cultured voice hesitantly entered the conversation.

Veronica saw a very elegant, beautifully made-up blonde in a casually tied headscarf wobble on high-heeled sandals across the uneven cobblestones on the pathway around the corner of the house, the upper part of her lovely face masked by outsized tortoiseshell sunglasses, her starkly plain black linen shift and oversized Fendi crocodile bag adding to the general air of studied fragility.

'Luc! Oh, Luc—thank God you're here!' She zeroed in on him like a heat-seeking missile, going on tiptoes to kiss his cheek, resting an exquisitely manicured hand on his chest.

'I'm so sorry if I'm barging in on your party, but I was just freaking out in your flat in London, and then I saw the news about you buying rings and I knew it was a sign I had to come down here and take charge of my life...' She clutched his arm, a semi-hysterical sob spilling from her ultra-pale pink lips as Luc quickly drew her to one side, to the relative privacy of his family's ranks.

'Oh, Luc, I'm such a total mess—but now I've done what you said—I've finally told Andrew I want a divorce. He tried to insist that we go to a counsellor, but I told him I was pregnant and that the baby most definitely wasn't his...'

Veronica felt the blood drain from her head and ice sink into the very marrow of her bones as she saw Luc take Elise Malcolm in his arms as she sobbed in earnest.

Not fragile, but desperate, she thought. The woman was on the verge of a total meltdown, and who could blame her?

'Oh, Luc, I do so want our baby but now I'm scared...what kind of parents will we make? I thought you might come back to Avignon with me and help me work it out…make everything right! I know you said I was on my own, but that was just your anger talking. Please, Luc, please—don't desert me when I need you the most!'

CHAPTER TEN

'PACKAGE for you, Veronica!'

Veronica looked up from her computer screen as her assistant called from the outer office.

'I'm off to my appointment in a few minutes,' she said, getting up to check her appearance in the mirror on the wall. 'Just check the invoice off with the order list and put it in with the other stock. I'll have a look when I get back.'

She was looking too pale, she thought, staring into her own haunted eyes. Even under a smooth coating of cosmetics her freckles looked more prominent on their translucent background and there were faint blue marks under her eyes that no amount of concealer could hide.

In the last two months the faint golden tan she had acquired in France had leached away, and, although they were now well into an Auckland spring, the long hours she had been working since her return meant that her body got little exposure to the sun. She had heard that lack of sunlight contributed to depression—there was even an official phrase for it: seasonal affective disorder—so perhaps that was the reason for the continued lethargy that dragged at her spirits in spite of the fact that her business was doing much better than she had expected. Lack of fresh air and the kind of daily exercise she was used to getting in the country could also explain her inability to sleep soundly and wretched moodiness.

Liar!

She glared at her wan face in the mirror. She knew very well what was causing her despondency, and it had nothing to do with a lack of sunlight.

'No, it's not for Out Of The Box,' said Carly. 'It's personal—for you.'

'Is it from Mum?' Her mother was always sending care-parcels of home-baking and organic produce—afraid that the big city would corrupt her into a fast-food lifestyle saturated with agri-chemicals.

'No, it's another one of *those*…'

Veronica froze, her heavy heart squeezing in her chest. She should just go—her appointment was with a new client and she didn't want to jeopardise her chance of an order by arriving late for their meeting.

Nevertheless, five minutes later she was opening the little box and lifting out a perfectly crafted, miniature shepherd-boy out of its bed of shredded green tissue.

'Oh, isn't he cute?' gushed Carly, who had been hovering with cheerful nosiness. Fresh out of university, she was a great worker, full of ideas and a whiz with the computer, and so eagerly interested in everything that Veronica had given up trying to preserve a businesslike distance between employer and employee. 'Now you'll have someone to put beside the lamb, and keep the old shepherd and his sheep company. What a pity it's only October—I wish it was Christmas already. I'm dying to see you put the whole crèche together!'

'Don't wish the Christmas rush on us just yet,' said Veronica croakily, her fingers smoothing over the glazed terracotta figurine. 'We still have an awful lot of work to get through before we're ready to ship off an avalanche of simultaneous orders…'

She turned the figure upside down to see the distinctive maker's mark on the base, although she didn't really need to look. She knew it came from Sénanque, as had each of the other five *santons* she'd received irregularly through the post over the past eight weeks.

She put the shepherd-boy back in its box with trembling fingers. Damn Luc! What on earth was he trying to do to her?

All the packages had arrived bearing a UK postmark and a customs sticker with his signature, but there was never any note inside so Veronica had no way of knowing what kind of message he was sending. If it was an apology it was a wretchedly cryptic one. Maybe it was just his way of rubbing her nose in her cowardice, but she had felt that his decision to leave for Avignon with Elise Malcolm in the middle of Zoe's party had been a fairly definitive statement of his priorities!

She snatched up her briefcase and slid in the laptop, and the glossy brochures and order forms, in case her potential client turned out to be electronically impaired. She had initially made a rule that, for the corporate side of the business, she wasn't going to pitch for business with companies that had less than twenty-five employees, but experience had quickly shown her the error of her ways. Many small companies valued their personal touch with their staff, and were more generous with gifts as rewards and incentives than larger organisations, and, besides, hungry small companies often mushroomed into big firms with many more clients and contacts. Sarron Holdings, according to her research, was a small but rapidly growing event-management company with contracts from a number of city councils and government organisations, as well as links with offshore promotions.

Picking up her handbag, she shot a furtive look at her assistant's back before tucking the new *santon* into the side pocket. Her personal talisman, a little piece of Luc to carry with her...

As she shot out the door her eye was caught by the card

propped up on the credenza. It had arrived the day before and she was still dithering about it—another reminder of that hedonistic, life-altering two weeks in Provence: a totally unexpected invitation to Sophie's twelfth birthday party the following week.

Waving to Carly, she sped out to her car, parked in one of the two spaces marked with the Out Of The Box logo in front of the long, rectangular building. Fortunately, it wouldn't take her more than fifteen minutes to get to the hotel where the meeting was to take place.

The series of disasters that had hit her immediately after she got back from France had helped distract her from her emotional trauma. The small warehouse she had previously arranged to lease was destroyed by a fire and the owner had decided not to rebuild, and the flat she had been poised to move into fell through, when the couple with whom she was going to share decided to go their separate ways. But then her real estate agent had offered her the rental of a 'work/life unit', a new concept of mixed-use development in an inner-city suburb, which comprised office and lock-up warehouse space downstairs and a spacious open-plan apartment above.

Veronica was living alone for the first time in her life…and the solitude gave her far too much time to brood on her sorrows. The only way she could bear it was to bury herself in work—hence her booming business.

The hotel was a downtown luxury high-rise overlooking Auckland's Waitemata Harbour, which at present was whipped up into white-caps by a passing spring squall. Veronica brushed the light rain spatters off her smart pale yellow linen suit as she entered the lift, her hopes regarding her new client rising with every floor, along with her nervous apprehension. She hadn't realised the room number she had been given was the penthouse suite. It indicated that Sarron Holdings might have a lot more money to spend than her initial research had led her to believe and she knew it was important not to show that she was intimidated. She would need to present a cool, confident front, no matter how much she might be quaking inside. But by now, she thought bitterly, she was practised at hiding her wayward emotions.

In the lobby, a bell-boy had inserted a security key to enable access to the top floor so she assumed that the front desk had called ahead, and was disconcerted when the lift door opened directly into the suite and there was no one to greet her.

She walked tentatively into the large room, elegantly furnished in creams and golds, the heels of her smart grey shoes, bought in a sale on the rue de Rivoli, clicking across the marble tiles in the open lobby before they sank into the deep pile of the luxurious carpet. The several doors that opened onto the room were all closed and she hesitated, clearing her throat.

When that tentative approach brought no response she walked over to the long cream couches that faced each other across a veined marble coffee-table, to put down her briefcase and handbag. Her eyes fell on the stack of newspapers on the coffee table she assumed were supplied by the hotel and her knees almost buckled.

The top one was an English broadsheet dated the previous day, and there on the front page was a photograph of a radiant Elise Malcolm laughing up at Max Foster at the Los Angeles première of his latest film, his big hand splayed over the distinct baby-bump revealed by her figure-hugging dress. An inset picture of a grim-looking older man whom the caption identified as Andrew Malcolm, who had released a statement the morning after the première that he had filed for a divorce from his wife on the grounds of adultery. No co-respondent was named in the divorce petition, but Malcolm had revealed that his wife was now living in Foster's Los Angeles home.

'I thought you'd like to see it hot off the presses—given your habit of relying on everyone's word but mine.' The dark, cynical words sliced through her heart, cutting off the oxygen supply to her brain.

With a virulent curse, Luc leapt forward as Veronica folded like a pack of cards, just managing to catch her up in his arms before her head hit the sharp corner of the table. Still cursing, he picked her up and laid her on the cream brocade couch, kneeling down to unbutton her jacket and comb her hair back from her milk-white face, tucking a cushion under her head and patting her cheeks.

'Veronica? Damn it, don't do this to me!'

Her eyes fluttered open and she stared up at him uncom-prehendingly.

'Where's Mr Atkinson?' she murmured, wildly disorientated.

Luc sat beside her, his hip hard against hers, his arm braced on the back of the couch above her prone body, his other hand smoothing her pleated brow.

'I don't know. Down in Wellington, I suppose, where he belongs,' he said gruffly. 'I own a big chunk of Sarron through a loan I made to Atkinson. Hence his lending me his name…'

Her brain was still processing information very slowly. 'But…we were going to talk business—'

His mouth compressed with impatience. 'I'll set up another meeting for you. Meantime, you and *I* are going to talk some long-overdue business!' The hand that had been tending her brow moved to plant itself flat on the cushion beside her face as he leaned close enough to snap her back into full awareness.

Her eyes flared with alarm and she licked her peach-glossed lips. 'I—could I have a drink of water?' she asked huskily.

But he had seen her eyes dart towards the lift. His jaw clenched. 'No.'

She noticed her open jacket, revealing her smooth camisole, and reached for her buttons, but he brushed her hands away.

'No distractions, or evasions. You're not budging from here until you start giving me some answers…about why you wouldn't take my calls, for a start! And why you didn't wait for me to come back from Avignon—I didn't expect to spend the night, let alone the next day as well, but I had a situation on my hands. I told you I'd explain everything as soon as I could.'

His eyes narrowed into fierce slits, his hand fisting on the back of the couch. 'But then, it seems you'd rather give everyone but me the benefit of the doubt. I thought that we'd established some rapport, that if you didn't trust me as a man, at least you respected who I was and you certainly seemed to like being with me, but then—' His jaw clamped down as he visibly fought the desire to roar, and she could practically see his tail lashing back and forth. 'God, Veronica—you really thought that I was sleeping with you while trying to hide from the consequences of having knocked up my adulterous lover! And on what evidence—'

'The evidence of my own eyes and ears!' she protested defensively. She knew it was weak. She had loved him, but she had lacked the courage, or the self-confidence, to fight for him. In her darkest moments, she had even wondered if the reason he hadn't rushed to return the engagement ring was because he had been keeping it for *that woman*…his first love, mother of his child—only, of course, she wasn't…

'But from whom? Not *me*. You didn't happen to notice that it was Elise who was doing all the talking and not making a lot of sense?' he echoed her thoughts acidly. 'I didn't have a chance to get a word in edgeways. She was hysterical, and working herself up into even more of a state. I thought the stress might hurt the baby if she kept it up—and by that I mean, *Foster's* baby, by the way,' he stressed with an incendiary glare, 'and she wasn't in any condition to drive back to Avignon by herself, let alone confront that arrogant son-of-a-bitch who was already roaring drunk when we finally ran him to ground—'

She was stricken with shame, with no excuse but blind, stupid jealousy. 'I didn't know—'

'No, of course you didn't! Melanie finally managed to get through to me to say you'd left to take up your original TGV booking, but I went to the station but by that time the train had left—'

He had gone to the station! And she had let him down—again—by not being there!

'I got there early and changed my ticket,' she admitted. She'd paid the premium gratefully, and then spent the whole six-and-a-half-hour journey in an agony of misery and uncertainty. As her searing hurt had faded she had begun to realise that she should have listened to Melanie's insistence that they had all got the wrong end of the stick, but then she had convinced herself that it was too late, he would never forgive her for her betrayal, not after all he'd been through.

'You really were desperate to get away from me, weren't you?' he said, his eyes branding her with his burning accusation. 'You left things in an uproar. Melanie and Miles thought I must have really hurt you to make you run away from me. I could have throttled you for making them think that of me—'

Her hand crept to her throat, though not out of fear. 'I'm sorry—' she whispered.

'About what?' he pounced.

She drank in the sight of him. In dark trousers and white shirt he looked lean and fit, but there were signs of strain around his eyes and mouth.

'You look tired—'

'So I should,' he said bitingly. 'I've been working like a slave for the past few weeks and spent the last twenty-four hours in the air without a wink of sleep.'

Veronica's searching eyes paused, and widened.

He tensed. 'What is it?'

She bit her lip. 'N-nothing.'

'It's not *nothing*. Start talking to me. It's the only way you're ever going to get out of here.'

But what if she didn't want to ever leave?

Luc was *here*, in *New Zealand*. He had gone to all this trouble to set her up for an ambush. Not the actions of a man who was intent on totally wiping her out of his life. Luc, too, needed closure.

'You have a couple of grey hairs…I never noticed them before,' she said, daring to touch the spot on his temple.

He recoiled, combing his fingers over the top of his head, almost dislodging the black band at the nape of his neck. 'That's because I never had any before. Not until I met you,' he added savagely. 'I'll probably be totally white by the time we're through.'

She propped herself up on her elbows as she realised what else was different. 'You're wearing a tie!'

He loosened the dark red silk self-consciously and unbuttoned his collar. 'I had a meeting with a couple of bankers this morning. I do know the principle of dressing to intimidate—'

'You mean, you haven't come all this way just to intimidate *me*.' She was beginning to recover her shattered composure, and more…she was beginning to see things from a perspective she had never before considered, put a different interpretation on his behaviour.

Now it was his turn to sound slightly defensive. 'I had to fill the time until you were due to arrive somehow.' He stood up. 'You're still looking a little pale—maybe you should have a glass of water.'

She had put him into retreat. She quickly scrambled off the couch in a panic. 'No, don't go—I'm fine. See!'

Her shoe brushed her handbag and it toppled over, the little terracotta shepherd-boy bounced out of the side pocket onto the carpet. They both bent to pick it up simultaneously, but Luc got there first.

He fingered it with startling tenderness as he straightened and looked at her, his eyes for the first time totally unguarded.

'You damned little fool!' he said roughly, the words encompassing everything that she had done…and not done.

She was shaken by the painful intensity in his voice and put her hand over his, needing the contact to get the words out: 'I'm sorry. I never meant to hurt you. I didn't realise I could—'

'How could you *not* know? God, even Gran could see I was crazy about you.' He raised their joined hands to his mouth. 'I thought I showed you how I felt—'

'A girl likes to be told,' she chided him, her smoky eyes shimmering with hope that her mistrust hadn't shattered his fundamental belief in *her*.

'So does a boy,' he said thickly. His fingers entwined with hers. 'I thought that when I put that ring on your finger in Avignon, that you might want to keep it there.'

For the second time that day her legs turned to jelly and this time he was ready. The tension lines on his face dissolved in a soft laugh as he sat with her on the couch and stood the shepherd-boy facing them on the coffee-table.

'A girl likes to be *asked*,' she said shyly.

'I thought it might frighten you off,' he said simply. 'For all the way we met, you're a cautious woman. I wanted to put my mark on you, but I didn't think you trusted me enough at that stage to say yes.'

And subsequent events had proved him right. She had never thought he lacked confidence, but in this one area he seemed as vulnerable as she had been—no wonder their tangle of emotions had become a snarl.

'I did wonder if you might want to keep it for Elise,' she confessed, and when his eyes flickered his distaste, she continued bravely, 'Well, you must admit, it was a very suspicious situation, and you never made any secret of the fact there was a lot more to the tale than you were telling.'

'Because it wasn't my tale to tell. I'd promised Elise absolute discretion, and I make a point of honouring my promises, even it they aren't easy to keep...*all* my promises,' he said quietly, with a look that made her warm all over. Suddenly she didn't want to talk—not about other people, anyway.

'Luc, I—'

'No, let's get this out of the way. Elise and Foster have got what they want, at the expense of a lot of pain to other people, so they at least owe you the truth.'

His gaze remained steady as he made no attempt to paint his actions in a heroic light, merely as a series of escalating complications—an honourable man trapped in a less than honourable situation.

'I wasn't having a meal with Elise the night of the fight, I was actually out at a formal dinner. She called me from Foster's hotel room in a panic. She said there was a photographer outside and Foster was drunk as well as high on something and threatening to make a scene, and she needed someone she could trust to help calm him down. Elise and I were better platonic friends than we were ever lovers, and I think she saw me as the only person whose discretion she could totally rely on—most of her other male friends were Andrew's political buddies or dependants. And I was already involved, although I didn't know it. Elise told me that night that the times Foster had stayed at my place in Derbyshire, she'd gone down there to be with him—they'd used me as a cover for their affair without having the courtesy to tell me about it.'

Veronica winced. No wonder he was touchy about personal loyalty. 'You still helped her, though—'

'Call me an old romantic,' he said wryly, 'but she *was* my first lover. She was also a politically helpful friend for many years. And I felt sorry for her—she'd got herself into a hell of a mess with someone whom I personally think is a walking disaster.

'Elise came downstairs at the hotel to meet me, but Foster followed her down and accused me of trying to break them up and that's when he attacked me. As soon as Elise realised someone had taken a photo of the fight, she knew they were in even worse trouble. If Foster's name was linked with hers, the press would be instantly all over them like a rash, whereas if it was my name it wouldn't attract so much attention and she still had true deniability: anyone digging for dirt about my relationship with her since her marriage was going to come up with zilch, because there was nothing to find. So we went to the restaurant to make it look like we were all having a sociable night out, and to try to talk some sense into Macho Man, and eventually we managed to convince him to go into rehab the next day, after which I was able to pour him back into his room. We were actually lucky the photos weren't used in the right order—it put a different spin on the story: a fight between two blokes over a social insult. Elise was in tears because Foster was accusing her of using him as a baby-factory. I advised her to tell Andrew straight away, before it hit the papers, and either ask for a divorce or ask him to accept the child as their own.'

'She could have pretended it was his baby…'

He gave her a dour look. 'Andrew's sterile.'

'Oh—'

'At that stage she still wasn't sure if she wanted to take the risk with Foster—she knows he's not a very stable person-ality, but I guess she must have decided he loves her enough to give up all his carousing for her and the baby. I let her stay in one of my company apartments after she moved out on Andrew, to lay low the press, but that was when she started thinking that she might be making a huge mistake. *My* mistake was letting her know I was going to be at St Romain with the family. I guess she just took it for granted that I would play the role of counsellor again when she burnt her boats and asked for the divorce. She nearly went back to London when she found old Max drunk as a skunk in Avignon, but he bounced back like an old pro the next day and claimed it was only because he'd been missing her and worrying she was having second thoughts. He can act, I'll give him that!'

'You certainly have some interesting friends,' murmured Veronica. She could almost feel sorry for Elise Malcolm.

'Who can go to the devil! At the moment I'm only interested in one, very particular friend,' he said, curving his hand under her chin and tilting up her face to slant his mouth over hers.

Quicksilver delight darted through her body as she put her hands against his crisp shirt-front. 'At the moment? That doesn't give us very long, does it?'

'A lifetime of moments,' he corrected himself, deepening the kiss to one of ravishing intimacy, his warm arms sliding under her jacket. 'I've worked day and night to free up enough time to come down here and convince you that you can trust me every moment of the rest of your life,' he said, nibbling along her jaw. 'I knew damned well *you* were never going to make the first approach...I sent you those *santons* as an advance guard, but I never heard a peep from you.'

'I was too ashamed,' she admitted, resting her forehead against his hard cheek. 'I thought being without you was my punishment for doubting your integrity. Deep down I don't think I did believe those things, but being in love was so overwhelming and all in only two weeks...I just got scared that I didn't know myself any more, let alone you...'

'Well, it's been a lot more than two weeks now, and if we're going to work out a deal I warn you I'm going to be a ruthless...' one hand slid up to cup her soft breast '...negotiator.'

She ached at his remembered touch. 'It's been so long...'

She felt his smile against her skin, warming her from the inside out. 'Have you forgotten how?' he teased.

She pulled her mouth away from his, for the sheer pleasure of pouting at him. 'To negotiate? I'm a businesswoman—it's what I do.'

To her disappointment he didn't immediately pull her back into his kiss.

'Then perhaps this will sweeten the deal.' He took the diamond ring she had worn so briefly from his pocket, holding it between his thumb and forefinger. 'Will you marry me, Veronica?' he said, with a formal sincerity that made the words sing in her heart.

She touched the rim of white fire. 'You want us to be boring and respectable, then?' she said, reminding him of his words in Avignon.

'Respectable, at least. Melanie would never forgive me if her grandchildren weren't legitimate, and Sophie said she won't let me come to her birthday party unless I bring you. Of course, Karen's not so hot on the idea of being my sister-in-law, but since she's going off on her modelling kick and I know a few people in the fashion industry she's decided there may be some advantages.'

She melted. 'You told them all…about us?'

He slid the ring on her slender finger with an expression of fierce satisfaction as he watched it settle home.

'I don't want any more secrets between us.'

'But I still have one,' she confessed gravely, looking at her hand in his, and the blaze of diamonds symbolising their new pact. She raised her eyes to his and his sudden tension eased as he saw they were laughing. 'You were right to be suspicious of me. I think I started falling in love with you the very first time I looked out of my window in Paris and saw you in that little café across the street. I spied on you for days, weaving dreams and plotting how to meet you, before I got up enough courage to actually do it.'

She tugged his red tie undone, stripping it from his collar and flinging it recklessly over the back of the couch. 'So you see, it wasn't fate, or coincidence, or your fantastic genius that brought us together. It was me!'

Her teasing laughter was smothered with kisses as he rose beautifully to the challenge.

'Then I suppose I should make one more confession, too.' He took out his wallet and extracted a folded blue square of paper, much creased. 'I was curious, so I picked your pocket in my bedroom at St Romain,' he disclosed shamelessly.

He carefully unfolded the square, but Veronica was already blushing at what she knew they would see.

'Even though you weren't ready to acknowledge it, you were for me. After you ran, it was my only proof.'

'Veronica Ryder' she had written several times in a soft, loopy signature with his beautiful sterling silver pen.

'I like the way it looks, don't you? But it sounds and tastes even better…' he murmured in her ear, taking her in his arms and settling down for a long, lazy loving with his heart's desire.

* * * * *

Here is a sneak preview of
A STONE CREEK CHRISTMAS,
the latest in Linda Lael Miller's acclaimed
McKETTRICK *series.*

A lonely horse brought vet Olivia O'Ballivan to Tanner
Quinn's farm, but it's the rancher's love that might cause
her to stay.

A STONE CREEK CHRISTMAS
Available December 2008
from Silhouette Special Edition

Tanner heard the rig roll in around sunset. Smiling, he wandered to the window. Watched as Olivia O'Ballivan climbed out of her Suburban, flung one defiant glance toward the house and started for the barn, the golden retriever trotting along behind her.

Taking his coat and hat down from the peg next to the back door, he put them on and went outside. He was used to being alone, even liked it, but keeping company with Doc O'Ballivan, bristly though she sometimes was, would provide a welcome diversion.

He gave her time to reach the horse Butterpie's stall, then walked into the barn.

The golden retriever came to greet him, all wagging tail and melting brown eyes, and he bent to stroke her soft, sturdy back. "Hey, there, dog," he said.

Sure enough, Olivia was in the stall, brushing Butterpie down and talking to her in a soft, soothing voice that touched something private inside Tanner and made him want to turn on one heel and beat it back to the house.

He'd be damned if he'd do it, though.

This was *his* ranch, *his* barn. Well-intentioned as she was, *Olivia* was the trespasser here, not him.

"She's still very upset," Olivia told him, without turning to look at him or slowing down with the brush.

Shiloh, always an easy horse to get along with, stood contentedly in his own stall, munching away on the feed Tanner had given him earlier. Butterpie, he noted, hadn't touched her supper as far as he could tell.

"Do you know anything at all about horses, Mr. Quinn?" Olivia asked.

He leaned against the stall door, the way he had the day before, and grinned. He'd practically been raised on horseback; he and Tessa had grown up on their grandmother's farm in the Texas hill country, after their folks divorced and went their separate ways, both of them too busy to bother with a couple of kids. "A few things," he said. "And I mean to call you Olivia, so you might as well return the favor and address me by my first name."

He watched as she took that in, dealt with it, decided on an approach. He'd have to wait and see what that turned out to be, but he didn't mind. It was a pleasure just watching Olivia O'Ballivan grooming a horse.

"All right, *Tanner*," she said. "This barn is a disgrace. When are you going to have the roof fixed? If it snows again, the hay will get wet and probably mold…"

He chuckled, shifted a little. He'd have a crew out there the following Monday morning to replace the roof and shore up the walls—he'd made the arrangements over a week before—but he felt no particular compunction to explain that. He was enjoying her ire too much; it made her color rise and her hair fly when she turned her head, and the faster breathing made her perfect breasts go up and down in an enticing rhythm. "What makes you so sure I'm a greenhorn?" he asked mildly, still leaning on the gate.

At last she looked straight at him, but she didn't move from

Butterpie's side. "Your hat, your boots—that fancy red truck you drive. I'll bet it's customized."

Tanner grinned. Adjusted his hat. "Are you telling me real cowboys don't drive red trucks?"

"There are lots of trucks around here," she said. "Some of them are red, and some of them are new. And *all* of them are splattered with mud or manure or both."

"Maybe I ought to put in a car wash, then," he teased. "Sounds like there's a market for one. Might be a good investment."

She softened, though not significantly, and spared him a cautious half smile, full of questions she probably wouldn't ask. "There's a good car wash in Indian Rock," she informed him. "People go there. It's only forty miles."

"Oh," he said with just a hint of mockery. "*Only* forty miles. Well, then. Guess I'd better dirty up my truck if I want to be taken seriously in these here parts. Scuff up my boots a bit, too, and maybe stomp on my hat a couple of times."

Her cheeks went a fetching shade of pink. "You are twisting what I said," she told him, brushing Butterpie again, her touch gentle but sure. "I meant…"

Tanner envied that little horse. Wished he had a furry hide, so he'd need brushing, too.

"You *meant* that I'm not a real cowboy," he said. "And you could be right. I've spent a lot of time on construction sites over the last few years, or in meetings where a hat and boots wouldn't be appropriate. Instead of digging out my old gear, once I decided to take this job, I just bought new."

"I bet you don't even *have* any old gear," she challenged, but she was smiling, albeit cautiously, as though she might withdraw into a disapproving frown at any second.

He took off his hat, extended it to her. "Here," he teased. "Rub that around in the muck until it suits you."

She laughed, and the sound—well, it caused a powerful and wholly unexpected shift inside him. Scared the hell out of him and, paradoxically, made him yearn to hear it again.

* * * * *

Discover how this rugged rancher's wanderlust is tamed in time for a merry Christmas, in
A STONE CREEK CHRISTMAS.
In stores December 2008.

™ *Silhouette*®

SPECIAL EDITION™

FROM *NEW YORK TIMES* BESTSELLING AUTHOR

LINDA LAEL MILLER

A STONE CREEK CHRISTMAS

Veterinarian Olivia O'Ballivan finds the animals in Stone Creek playing Cupid between her and Tanner Quinn. Even Tanner's daughter, Sophie, is eager to play matchmaker. With everyone conspiring against them and the holiday season fast approaching, Tanner and Olivia may just get everything they want for Christmas after all!

Available December 2008
wherever books are sold.

Virgin Brides, Arrogant Husbands

Demure but defiant...
Can three international playboys
tame their disobedient brides?

Proud, masculine and passionate, these men
are used to having it all. But enter Ophelia,
Abbey and Molly, three feisty virgins to whom
their wealth and power mean little. In stories
filled with drama, desire and secrets of the
past, find out how these arrogant husbands
capture their hearts....

Available in December

THE GREEK TYCOON'S
DISOBEDIENT BRIDE
#2779

REQUEST YOUR FREE BOOKS!

2 FREE NOVELS PLUS 2 FREE GIFTS!

PASSION GUARANTEED SEDUCTION

HP08R